NO PENALTY
FOR LOVE

NO PENALTY
FOR LOVE

•

Shellie Foltz

09-468

AVALON BOOKS
NEW YORK

Published by Thomas Bouregy & Co., Inc.
160 Madison Avenue, New York, NY 10016

Library of Congress Cataloging-in-Publication Data

Foltz, Shellie.
   No penalty for love / Shellie Foltz.
      p. cm.
   ISBN 978-0-8034-9975-1 (hardcover : acid-free paper)
   I. Title.
   PS3606.O54N6   2009
   813'.6—dc22

                                   2009012799

PRINTED IN THE UNITED STATES OF AMERICA
ON ACID-FREE PAPER
BY HADDON CRAFTSMEN, BLOOMSBURG, PENNSYLVANIA

To my husband and family for your love, encouragement, and enthusiasm. You have always made a place for my writing—this one's for you (at last)! You are God's blessing in my life.

I would like to acknowledge the following teachers for their valuable instruction and their encouragement as I grew in my craft: Mrs. Joyce Pyle, Mrs. Lois Dugan, Mrs. Velma Null, and Mrs. Betty Nicholson.

Thanks also to the Missouri State University Ice Bears for bringing the sport to my hometown. Go Bears!

Chapter One

In every schoolteacher's life there comes a time when she must determine that the world is either worth saving or it isn't. If it isn't, she must decide if the premature death she is bound to suffer as a result of stroke brought on by high blood pressure brought on by the boy in fifth period who consistently interrupts her lectures with brilliant insights such as "That's lame" is more or less painful than abandoning the career she believed in—the career she is still paying student loans for and has grown disillusioned by. If it is more painful to give it up, then she must decide how she will make the days more bearable. Will she:

A) randomly write "That's lame" in the margins of the research essays she brought home to grade over spring break?

1

B) become a drinker?

C) take on an extracurricular sponsorship in hopes of rekindling her passion for youth? Or,

D) keep a private calendar under the blotter on her desk with a running count of school days remaining until June and a collection of color photos clipped from travel brochures?

After seriously considering B and even investing in a beginner's set of home bar accessories and those very cute wine glass tags based on Monopoly game pieces which are designed to help disoriented guests keep track of their drinks, I picked up a brochure from a travel agency and committed, at least for this academic year, to answer D and to the Mediterranean.

Every day, Monday through Friday beginning September 1, as soon as fifth period dismissed I stole a peek at the cornflower-blue waters and the blinding white sands and domed roofs of Greece. Then, I took a miniature box of raisins from the top right-hand drawer and told myself that I would be glad I foreswore the Snickers bar when, come June, I would be wearing my new swimsuit and floating, carefree, in that sea of myths and miracles.

Christmas break was coming, too, which is always a marker in the public scholar's path. One semester ends. Another begins. In between there is a block of weeks in which I cease to be Miss Smythe, professional educator, and become again that Patricia of long ago: The one who read for pleasure and who wrote for the thrill of it, who when she saw a movie was either enchanted by the characters or disdainful of the storyline and whose first thoughts upon departing the cinema were not, "If I buy the DVD when it comes out I could show that scene with the white dress and the red flowers to my juniors as an example of symbolism." Teaching really is hazardous to your health.

Or, at least it is hazardous to your mental health.

In the eight years I'd been teaching "tomorrow's hope" the difference between Steinbeck's use of gritty language in *Of Mice and Men* and the use of vulgarities in the hallway, I changed. My personal pedagogy eroded under the force of nature which is the public school. I wasn't rock-solid anymore. I was worn out.

I attended workshops on enhancing resiliency in students and wondered where my own snap had gone. It eloped with the elasticity in my skin somewhere around my thirtieth birthday, I supposed. Still, I pressed on toward the major instructional goals of my American and British literature courses with the public school district's mission and vision statements memorized for recitation upon request of an administrator doing a classroom walkthrough. Dutiful, focused, I prepared students for the state assessment. I made sure that no child was left behind. I planned. I explained. I challenged. I supported. I assessed. I went home.

At night, I stepped onto one of two uncomfortably comfortable and well-worn paths: Inhaling junk food until dinner was on the table or napping in front of the television until sunset. I tried going for a workout instead of going home, or taking papers to the local coffeehouse to grade. The rut was too deep, however. I found I was settled in the routines which shaped me, rather than the other way around. I was staring vacantly at the calendar under my blotter, calculating days and dollars (which always seem to be in short supply), and hearing students approaching the door. I had become mesmerized by the repetition of the days. I was bored.

"Miss Smythe?" a male voice asked hesitantly.

It was too mature a voice to be a student. Not an administrator—I know those voices well, I hear them in my sleep. It was a deep voice filled with life. The kind I heard in my dreams. I knew this before looking up and hearing my own breath catch in my throat like that of a child with her hand caught in the proverbial cookie jar. I let go of the blotter and straightened my shoulders, turned my head toward the visitor and rose in one fluid motion of feigned professionalism. "Yes?" I heard myself say. Did my voice crack? "I'm Miss Smythe. May I help you?"

His chest was broad, an expanse of open beach waiting to be explored inch by inch. The reason I noticed his chest first was not that I was hungry for male companionship—which I was—nor was it that his chest was right at eye level for me, which it was. Rather, the reason I noticed his chest first was this: As a heightened security measure, our district adopted identification badges. I tried not to think about the reasons for wearing the badge as I draped the purple and gold lanyard around my neck each morning. I trusted my students and could not continue in my profession if I found I feared them. I check for the badge instinctively now. His chest *was* broad. VISITOR the tag said.

"I'm Josh Northshore." He extended his mitt-sized hand toward me.

"Abel's father?" I asked hesitantly, thinking immediately that he was too young to be the father of an eighteen-year-old and approaching him slowly, suddenly hyperaware of how loudly my heels sounded on the old floor tiles.

"Could be, but no. I'm his older brother." He smiled and clasped my hand. "And guardian."

"I have a class coming just now, Mr. Northshore. If you can wait just a few minutes, I'll get them started on their assignments and then we can talk." I felt color rising inexplicably to my face.

"Sure," he said, offhandedly and obviously not used to being put off. "May I wait here?" He gestured to a chair next to my desk.

"Of course," I answered lightly though I was filled with reluctance. He'll be watching me teach. I panicked. This is private time for me and my students. Nobody ever comes through so closely to bell. Teachers may find themselves micromanaged these days, but etiquette dictates that the first few moments of class are sacred.

Josh Northshore. Josh Northshore. Why is that name so familiar?

"Josh Northshore!" I heard Kevin Lazarus shout as he entered the room with his usual bluster. "Awesome play last night!" Kevin headed past me and straight to my guest.

"Thanks." Josh Northshore stood and took the boy's hand in his own, engulfing it. "Were you there?"

"Working concessions. Fundraiser for my kid sister's dance team. They get like one dollar for every twenty-five dollars sold or something like that," he explained with a shrug. "Bunch of screaming, giggling ten-year-old tap dancers." He waved the thought of them away like a pesky gnat hovering around his nose.

Hockey! That's it! Josh Northshore is a Showboats player. "Kevin, take your seat, please," I heard myself saying. "The bell's just about to ring."

The room had filled up with jabbering juniors. No one was seated and the bell could hardly be heard over the noise. "Seats, please!" I shouted to be heard.

"Is Mr. Northshore our guest speaker?" Travis asked, sliding into his chair.

"All right!" someone shouted. "A guest speaker! Free day!"

"Can we ask any kind of questions we want?" a too-heavily made-up sixteen-year-old asked in a tone too suggestive to be ignored.

I looked quickly at the handsome blond star sitting uncomfortably on the rickety wooden school-issue chair.

His discomfort settled across his face and his eyes dropped to the floor. Was he embarrassed? I was.

"No." I shook my head. "No, Mr. Northshore is here to talk with me. So, in the meantime, I want you to get out your books"—I was interrupted by a groaning which suggested I had sentenced them to death by easy listening tunes installed on their personal music lists—"and turn to page three-twenty-eight. There you will find an excerpt from Mark Twain's *Life on the Mississippi.* Yesterday, we talked about organization of a piece of writing. We had two mental models. Who recalls?" I asked hopefully. A delicate hand appeared at the back. "Lindsay?" I acknowledged her gratefully.

"Big picture to little picture and little picture to big picture," Lindsay answered.

"Correct. Note as you read that Twain uses both of these techniques of organization in his descriptions of the river and of the cub pilot's *perception* of the river. Note line numbers where you find Twain using these techniques and we'll create some non-linguistic representations later this period. Any questions?"

"Do we get to color?"

"If you catch all of the descriptions, you may color your graphics when you finish," I replied in my practiced tenor of mild condescension mixed with vague amusement. It works. "Anything else?"

There was no response other than what I expected. About ten out of thirty-three had already begun reading. Another five had closed their books. Two never opened them to begin with. The rest were turning pages to see how long the selection was, looking at the ceiling, drawing on the desks or heading my way for restroom passes. I headed them off.

"I will only give green passes after I've seen you making real efforts toward the assignment." Another groan. I turned to the handsome hockey hero, Mr. Northshore.

"Shall we step into the hall?" I asked politely. Hallway chats provide their own special brand of intimacy.

He stood and followed me to the door. I allowed him to go by, taking him in, admiring his form as he passed. I turned to my class and gave them a look before exiting.

"What can I do for you?" I asked, perhaps a bit too brightly.

"I'm here about Abel. I understand it's questionable as to whether or not he will pass this semester."

"I'm afraid there's not much question about it." I smothered my sarcasm. Abel Northshore had been the thorn in my side all semester. "It's too bad, Mr. Northshore . . ."

"Josh, please." He smiled.

"It's too bad, Josh, that you weren't able to come to conference two weeks ago. I did try to phone to let you know that Abel had failed to complete his research assignment. That, unfortunately, was worth about twenty percent of his entire semester grade."

"For one assignment?" Josh was flabbergasted.

"It took about four weeks, which is a healthy chunk

of the semester," I answered calmly, resenting the need for explanation even as I gave one.

"I was out of town with the team. Is there anything we can do to fix it?" He scratched his head, searching for a solution. "We have a home stand the next two weekends." He leaned toward me. Was he trying to intimidate or seduce?

"I'm afraid not. Abel knew what the assignment was worth well in advance and still chose not to do it. That is the biggest problem. However, Abel's grade would still be in trouble had he done the research assignment. His work ethic leaves something to be desired. I only receive about one of every three or four assignments from him. I realize you're on the road with your team." I smiled disarmingly. "Is there someone at home to help Abel?" *Please, say no. Please say no.*

"Mrs. Flannery is there but I'm afraid she's not much help. She'll be leaving for Christmas with her family. Ireland," he was thinking aloud. "When does the semester actually end?" He was embarrassed that he didn't know.

"The semester ends after mid-terms when we return from winter break."

"Could he catch up on those other assignments and turn them in after the break?" He raised his eyebrows, daring me to refuse.

"Mr. Northshore—"

"Josh," he corrected, and touched my arm.

I was beginning to feel warm. "Josh, it isn't just a

matter of catching up. These assignments are meant as practice of the skills we are learning in class. It isn't just about points."

"It is where I work." He grinned.

"Yes." I smiled back. "However, your coach wouldn't put up with you showing up for every third or fourth practice would he? I mean, you couldn't possibly be playing your best game that way. Could you?" *Oh, no! Did that sound patronizing?*

"No, I wouldn't be at my best. I see what you're saying, Miss Smythe . . ."

He lingered on my name. *Is he wanting me to permit a more familiar use of my first name as he had?* "Miss Smythe. I know Abel is a bit of a pain sometimes"—he hesitated again, I smiled—"but, I'm really working hard to get him back on track. Sometimes a kid just needs a break. Do you know what I'm saying?"

"I understand that, Josh, but is it fair to the other students in the class who put in their time and effort that Abel should walk away with the same grade for putting in a few hours over break and slap-dashing off a few late assignments? I hardly think so."

"Look, I'm not asking you to give him anything he doesn't earn. I'm just asking you to let him have a second chance to earn it."

"This requires a lot of me, Josh. I would have to get all of the past assignments together and then obligate myself to grade them at the last minute even as I'm scoring mid-term exams."

"I understand." He nodded, his eyes downcast. "Thank you for your time, Miss Smythe."

He turned to go. I watched him heading for the stairs. He was tall and muscular, angular and sexy. I felt myself growing vaguely dizzy and shook my head to recover. He turned suddenly on his heels and stepped back toward me, covering the same floor area in about half as many steps. "I have an idea," he announced, standing toe to toe with me.

Bargaining has never been one of my strong suits. I felt the air go out of me like a popped balloon. "Yes?" I asked, suspiciously.

"What if I hired you?"

"I'm not looking for a second job," I said flatly.

"Not permanently. Just over the break." His speech sped up with excitement.

I shook my head free of its lust-induced fuzziness and forced myself to hear what he was saying.

"Mrs. Flannery is going to Ireland for Christmas. I was going to have to hire someone to watch Abel anyway. We're going on the road. The break's over two weeks. If you would come along and work just on English with Abel one-on-one every day during that time, that would surely make up for the hours he's wasted in class and let him really *earn* his grade. What do you say?"

He held out his hand as if the offer lay in his palm.

"Excuse me?" I was bewildered.

"You come along with Abel and the team. Spend the

days teaching him and helping him make up his work. Sorry, earn his grade. At night, free admission to the games or whatever you want."

"I'm not accustomed to babysitting my students," I answered, trying not to sound completely insulted, though I was.

"I'm sorry. Of course. It's your holiday too. I'm sure you have plans with family? Friends? A vacation you've already planned?"

When I didn't respond right away, he seemed encouraged. "I would pay you one hundred dollars a day, Monday through Friday. Plus your room and board while we're gone. I can't leave Abel at home unattended, Miss Smythe"—his voice had taken on a pleading quality— "I don't know how much you know about what's been going on with Abel outside of school this year, but we're just turning a corner. I really think that this chance, this show of confidence, could be a real help. Would you consider it? Please?"

"I don't know what to say." My mind was reeling. How could I agree to such a preposterous plan? Tutoring students for a fee was not unheard of. A teacher's time is her own beyond contract hours. Still, something felt weird with the whole setup.

While I weighed my options, Josh reached into his hip pocket and pulled out his wallet. "Here," he said, handing me his card with the raised Showboat Wheel in the upper right corner. "Consider it, Miss Smythe." He appealed to me earnestly as he scrawled something on the back of the card. "My home number. Call me when you've decided."

He turned to go but stopped. I looked up into his eyes, noticing for the first time the deep, sparkling blue. Sapphires set handsomely. His hand was extended again. "Thank you for your time and your consideration. I'll defer to your professional judgment. I know you want what's best for your students. Despite everything, Abel tells me you really care about the kids. If you're willing to meet him halfway on this, I'll be very much in your debt. Well beyond what I could pay you."

I took his hand. My mind was numb. I couldn't speak. He turned to leave. I leaned against the cold lockers and tried to differentiate between the sound of his footsteps in the stairwell and the unsettling pounding of my heart.

"Miss Smythe?" The voice struggled to get through to me. "Miss Smythe?" The voice came again.

"You can call me Patricia," I answered, weakly.

"What?"

"Patricia."

"Are you okay?"

I turned dreamily and saw Veronica Williams standing there with her neon-pink hair and nose ring.

"I really need to go to the bathroom, Miss Smythe. I've finished the reading."

Writing a hall pass for Veronica, I realized I suddenly had no recollection of the details of Twain's essay, and hurriedly reread the piece as the ten who began on time finished up, the seven who never started slept, and the rest began turning pages at random and scanning them for the required information. Suddenly, the passionate yet poignant observations of a cub pilot paled in comparison to the life-sized hockey star who had just walked out of my life.

At 2:45 the bell rang to dismiss school. In less time than it takes a spit wad to find its way from the end of a straw to the classroom ceiling, Miss Cherrie Ramsey was standing in my doorway.

"Who was that?" she gushed, seating herself at my desk.

"Who?" I asked as casually as I could, turning my back to erase what was quite possibly the last remaining chalkboard in the school system. "Do you think we'll really get the upgrades next year? I'm pretty sure I'm getting the teacher equivalent of black lung from all this chalkdust."

"Don't be coy with me, Patricia. Who was he?"

"Oh, Abel's brother, you mean?" I struck upon what I thought would register as an expression falling somewhere in the range of disinterest to amused accusation. "Why do you ask?"

"Why do I ask? Why do I ask?" She took me by the shoulders and shook me roughly. "Do you need new glasses? Or have you decided upon a celibate lifestyle?"

"Okay, okay." I laughed. "Kind of handsome, isn't he?"

"No kind of about it," she sat again. "I swear my ticker was ticking in double time just looking at him."

Cherrie was nearing forty and had never been married. Her ticker was not her heart but her biological clock. After having taught high school for so many years, I would have thought that such strong maternal urges would have been tempered by good common sense, but not for Cherrie. Her unrelenting desire for babies was widely known and remarked upon. Cherrie had been the butt of many jokes among faculty and had received numerous alarmingly authentic-looking coupons for herbal supplements formulated to extend the reproductive years well into the sixties. Cherrie never mentioned receiving them, even to those on staff who consider themselves her friends; this fact alone caused a little too much speculation into Miss Ramsey's quest for the positive pregnancy test.

I was Cherrie's friend and though I only ever heard of these tasteless gags through others on staff, never from Cherrie herself, I knew she was bound and determined that she would have children the old-fashioned way. She was quite traditional.

"Okay, I admit it, he was very handsome," I relented and her consternation vanished like a shadow in the noonday sun.

"Thank you," she said with satisfaction. "So, you up for a cappuccino?"

"Sure. Give me ten minutes, okay? I need to check my e-mail and make a phone call."

Cherrie and I favored a local coffee shop in the Central West End just a few blocks from the antiques district.

It was the opposite direction of home, but once in a while it was nice. Besides, it gave me a chance to check in with Zenobia, the barista-astrologer-greeting-card-verse writer who seemed to be there serving up flavored steamed milks and coffees at all hours. The last time I spoke with her, she told me that the pivotal time for love was when the moon was crescent and three ladies danced, or something equally bizarre sounding. I thanked her for her insight and left a generous tip in the jar.

Zenobia was working this afternoon, and as Cherrie and I walked in she was singing in a foreign language to some Middle Eastern-sounding music. Cherrie rolled her eyes. Though I cannot be considered by any stretch of the imagination to be peculiar, eclectic, or even plain unconventional, I am not, I hope, nearly as provincial as Cherrie. I, at least, appreciate the individualism on display in this city of ours. I have often considered giving up my little ranch-style home in the suburbs and renting a loft or something downtown. My healthy sense of practicality precludes such a move, though.

"It's her again." Cherrie forced the statement through her teeth.

"Oh, she's fun," I said as I nudged my colleague with my elbow. "Hey, Zenobia," I chirped a little too brightly in compensation for my drinking buddy. "What's new today?"

"Come taste." Zenobia waved me over to the counter. I pushed Cherrie ahead of me. "It's a fair trade blend.

Really yummy." She offered us two thimble-sized cardboard cups. "Smooth, huh?" She raised her eyebrows and opened her eyes wide awaiting our response.

"Yummy," I agreed. "I think I'll have one. What's it called?"

"Golden Rain," she answered dreamily.

"Golden Rain? Why?" I never buy a lipstick or nail polish with a plain name or only a number when I can get something exotic sounding instead. Why settle for "dark roast" when you can have "Golden Rain?"

"Oh, read the story." She slapped a laminated narrative on the counter for me to peruse. "It's fascinating. Plus, it makes you feel good to know you're helping someone somewhere earn a decent living by choosing this coffee over another one."

Cherrie interrupted. "I think I'll have a decaf cappuccino with a squirt of amaretto," she stated flatly in her usual authoritative and curt tone.

I felt embarrassed by Cherrie's staid attitude and began reading the descriptions of the coffees on the card to distance myself a little. I cared that Zenobia knew I was not a stick-in-the-mud like my colleague. I dreaded the idea of becoming dull. I didn't want the company I kept to give people the wrong impression of me.

After two cups of Golden Rain, I drove home with Josh Northshore's card propped up on the dashboard. I ran a stoplight and missed my exit before finally arriving at my modest home in St. Charles just as a few snowflakes began to blow across the hood of the car.

Pulling into the drive, I was tempted to spend the evening in a Thomas Kincaid kind of mindset: The world is pretty inside and out; the holidays are coming and snow is fluttering about; the fire is burning brightly and I'm so glad I went ahead and put out a few lights in the boxwood. But my eyes were drawn instead to my grandmother's custom red Land Rover with leopard-print upholstery parked under my carport, and her teacup poodle, Bitsy, decked out in a green and red sweater with a holly sprig wired into her topknot, tied to a tree and yapping incessantly.

"Oh, no," I heard myself whisper and immediately shamed myself for feeling intruded upon.

Nanna is my mother's mother. She is spry and vibrant. She is everything I hope to be when I'm old even though I'm none of those things now. She behaves like a kid in college. She has groups of friends. She goes gambling and dancing. She e-mails and shops online. My grandmother takes a class called Dating After Fifty and often dines with spunky old men at unusual little bistros in downtown St. Louis. I envy her. I love her, but at this moment I was not so happy to find her here. Thoughts of Josh Northshore, his impressive span of muscular chest, his mesmerizing eyes, and his offer drifted further from the reaches of my imagination with each of Bitsy's yaps. Nanna appeared in the doorway waving. She was wearing hot-pink tights with a chartreuse V-neck sweater and had a Christmas-printed kerchief knotted at her neck.

"I made pumpkin chili," she announced as I came into my living room, lugging with me several hours' worth of assignments to grade.

"Pumpkin chili?" I asked, dropping my bags and dusting snow from my shoulder.

"Is it snowing?" She pushed past me back to the door and hurried outside to untie her dog. "Come inside, Bitsy! Oh, isn't it pretty, Patricia?"

"Yes. I thought you were coming tomorrow night?"

"I was." She set Bitsy on the carpet and helped her out of her sweater. "But Mr. Evanston asked me to the chocolate bar tomorrow night."

"Who's Mr. Evanston?" I made my way to the kitchen. "And what is pumpkin chili?"

"Chili with pumpkin in it," she said rather offhandedly. "Mr. Evanston is the attorney who handled your mother's will. He's in my dating class." She grinned and took the lid from the large pot on my stove.

Nanna is a messy cook. I scanned the kitchen for damage. All the evidence was there: Meat wrapper, several bottles of spices with the lids scattered far and wide, onion peel, and a can of puréed pumpkin scraped clean and left with its jagged lid standing open.

"Taste." She shoved a wooden spoon at me.

"Hot," I said around the mouthful.

"But good, isn't it? I got the recipe off the Internet," she offered without waiting for my reaction. "Pumpkin is very good for you."

"Shall I set the table?" I asked politely.

"I'll do that. You go on and get changed. You look flushed. Are you feeling well?"

My grandmother's brand of conversation is often rapid-fire. I nodded politely and made my way down the hall to my bedroom. The smell of the chili followed me. I closed the door in vain.

My room, indeed, my whole house, is messy. I don't want it to be but it is. Everywhere there are piles of books and papers, unfinished projects that I meant to get back to the next day and that will go undone for several months longer. I turned on the television and undressed. The weatherman was forecasting several inches of snow when I caught my reflection in the full-length mirror and, despite my first instinct, decided to take a good look. I am taller than most women in my family at five-foot-five. I weigh more than I think I should, but seem to carry it well, like a curvaceous starlet from the 40s or 50s. I'm not unattractive. I swept my annoyingly wavy brown hair back from my face with the intent of pulling it into a ponytail when I noticed something that really disgusted me. I was wearing my mother's underwear. Not literally my mother's underwear, but the kind I remember seeing her wear: White cotton briefs and a functional crisscross bra with wider "comfort straps." My jaw dropped. I let my hair go and stared. I turned to the side and stared some more. I turned again and looked back over my shoulder. When did this happen? When did I start assuming that the standard for my choice of underpinnings was practicality? I reached for my jeans and sweatshirt hurriedly and vowed to sort through my unmentionables later when Nanna left in an effort to reestablish some definition of myself as a sexual being.

I wouldn't want to give the impression that I have been—or intend to become—promiscuous. I haven't and don't. But that never prevented me in my younger days from giving consideration to how a certain pair of lacy panties or a certain black plunge bra made me feel.

I'll bet Nanna wears sexier underwear, I thought as I turned off the television and pulled on a pair of socks. *She probably gets pedicures, too,* I considered as I noted the sad state of my toenails. *I'll paint them later.* I wondered if I had any nail lacquer that hadn't solidified from disuse.

Nanna called. Dinner was on the table: Big, steaming bowls of thick, burnt-orange stew accompanied by crusty bread and a field greens salad with oil and vinegar and glasses of cold milk.

Thoughts of Josh returned as I warmed up and began to ease into the comfort of home and family. "I received a proposition today, Nanna," I said casually.

"Was it an indecent one?" She leaned forward hopefully, a youthful glint in her eye.

"No." I laughed.

"Oh." She was disappointed and resumed her dinner.

"It was unusual, though." I didn't wish to disappoint her. She laid her spoon aside to give me her full attention. "From a hockey player."

"Oh, I love hockey players," she gushed and fanned her face rapidly.

"Nanna!"

"What? I dated a hockey player once. Two of them, actually." She crossed her arms, daring me to question the sincerity of the claim. "At the same time," she added, goading me.

"Fine. Anyway, he wanted me to go along with the team over the break."

"You're going aren't you?" she nearly scolded, anticipating my boring yet profoundly sensible answer.

"I haven't decided yet, as a matter of fact." I raised an eyebrow, trying to match her capacity for suggestiveness. She shrugged as if disinterested. I let it simmer.

"Okay, what hockey player was it and what does he want you to *do* on this trip?" Nanna asked in her amateurish attempt at propriety.

I smiled. I'd won. Finally! "Josh Northshore." I hesitated to see if she knew him.

"Hunky, I'm impressed."

Another point in my column. "I have his younger brother in class," I explained, feeling my triumph waning even as I spoke. "He wants me to go along to help Abel catch up on some missing work." My voice faded to nothing near the end of my explanation. "It's nothing, really," I finished off and quickly scooped up a big bite of chili to stop myself from saying anything more.

"Oh." She sounded disappointed. "Well," she began hopefully, but let the thought remain unfinished.

"Well, what?" I wished with all my might that she would encourage me to go along, would feed the adolescent fantasy that had just begun to form.

"You could go. It's legal, isn't it?"

"Of course it's legal. Would I do something illegal?"

"Is it moral?" she goaded.

"Nanna." I was becoming exasperated.

"Well," she began again, shrugging.

"What is that supposed to mean?" I crossed my arms in front of me.

"Just that you never know what could happen."

That was it. That was the most optimistic supposition she could make. "No, you never know," I repeated, effectively sealing the opening on that particular topic.

Nanna stayed until it was too late for me to grade papers with any semblance of concentration. I turned on the lights in the boxwoods and flicked on the gas log in the fireplace. I started to turn on the late movie but caught my reflection in the still-blank screen and felt a creeping sense of guilt. A promise is a promise. I turned off the fire and padded down the hallway to my bedroom.

I picked up the business card Josh had given me and let my finger run over the raised impression of the Showboats' insignia and trail along the full length of his name: JOSIAH N NORTHSHORE, RIGHT WING. I let my mind roam briefly to the Mediterranean, my favorite pastime of late. There I stretch out on a blanket under the warm sun, the brilliance of the white sand nearly blinding me. I turn to get a book from my beach bag and my hand meets his. Suddenly, the collection of critical essays on Charlotte Perkins Gillman seems as irrelevant as last year's class roster. I drop the book back into the bag and turn my palm up. His lips part and his eyelids become heavy with longing. He raises my wrist to his mouth and I can feel his hot breath tickle the tender flesh. I hear a catch in my throat and his name is in my breath.

Then, the phone rang.

Sitting amidst a seemingly endless expanse of white underwear, I searched for the handset. "Hello?" *Is my voice raspy?*

"Miss Smythe?"

My mind raced. My students don't have my home number and I'm not listed in the directory. I had recently been added to the state's no-call list. Who was this?

"Miss Smythe?"

I pinched my leg and chastised myself for not checking the caller identification before answering. "Yes," I responded hesitantly. "This is Patricia Smythe. Who's calling?"

"Josh Northshore." I went numb. "Listen, I'm sorry to call you at home. I've just been thinking about you this evening. I wondered if you have had a chance to consider our little"—he searched for the right word— "well, my little offer?"

"Actually, Mr. Northshore." I was feeling simultaneously piqued and eager—he had been thinking about me.

"Josh, please." I could almost hear the mischievous grin in his voice.

"Josh, I've had company this evening and haven't had the opportunity to consider it further." My fingers found the business card and I looked at it, trying to picture his face behind the printed name. "I can say, however, that I find it a most unusual . . ."

"Offer?"

"Offer. And, while I'm certainly interested in seeing Abel earn his credit, I can't say that I see this as a real possibility."

"What can I do to help make it a real possibility?" the professional athlete with the never-say-die attitude asked.

I melted. He sounded so genuine, so desperate. There hadn't been many times in my life when I was the one holding the reins. I found I rather liked it.

"I don't know what teachers make, you see," he stammered. "If the amount I quoted to you was less than professional, I'd be happy to raise it to a more appropriate level."

"It's not the money," I said flatly. Teachers' salaries are always a touchy subject. "It's simply a matter of my personal time being valuable to me and the idea of cramming in a whole semester's worth of work into a mere two weeks. It just doesn't seem right to me."

"Look, Miss Smythe," he said in a more businesslike tenor.

"Patricia," I gave him permission softly.

"Patricia," he repeated it as softly; I could hear the smile in his voice. "That's a nice name. An old name. Not many people name their little girls Patricia these days. Do they?"

"No, I don't suppose they do." I didn't know any other Patricias under fifty.

"Patricia, I really need help. It seemed logical to me to go straight to the source. You know Abel. You know what his abilities are and where he needs help. He holds you in high regard, as I told you earlier today. Because I respect that what I'm asking you to do encroaches on your very valuable time away from work, I won't sink to bribery, but I will say that if there is anything at all beyond what we have already discussed that would make this more"—again, he searched for the right word— "palatable, I would be happy to hear it. Other than that, I can promise you Abel will be angelic; and, road trips can be a lot of fun. Think of it as an adventure. A Christmas adventure. Will you let me know?"

"I'll think about it, Josh." I found I liked saying his name. "I'll make a decision and get back to you this week. Is that soon enough?"

"Thank you," he nearly whispered.

I sat mute listening to his easy breathing over the line.

"Good night, Patricia," his tone was altered somehow, distant, pensive. "I'll talk to you soon."

"Good night, Josh." I hung up the phone and held the handset for a long time, staring at it and running my thumb along the edge as if it was Josh's strong jawline. "Good night, Josh," I whispered again, as I sank into a deep slumber on the soft sands, which somehow resemble piles of white cotton underwear.

Chapter Two

I forgot to set the alarm. When I woke up, my first thought was, *How did he get my number?* My second thought was, *First period starts in forty-five minutes!* I turned on the radio and raced for the bathroom as the announcer continued the headline story.

". . . overnight with snows amounting to six inches throughout the county. Traffic has come to a standstill on I-forty-four. Road crews worked throughout the night but were unable to keep up with this wicked winter storm. We'll have our updated school closings list next."

I peeked through the curtains. The snow had come down hard. I had forgotten to shut off the Christmas lights in the shrubs and they glowed like fireflies in a misty forest underneath their chilly blanket. I raced back to my bedroom when I heard the commercials end.

"St. Louis and surrounding suburbs, you are out of school today! Turn over and go back to sleep!"

"Yes!" I pumped my fist over my head joyously. Snow days are one of the great pleasures of being a teacher. While the rest of the world digs out and presses on, I get to drink an extra cup of coffee and read the paper, stay in my robe all day long, bake cookies and watch whatever mind-numbing show happens to be on TV.

However, after finishing a whole pot of coffee, eating five peanut butter cookies—not counting the unbaked spoonfuls I helped myself to between batches—and watching three episodes of "Leave It to Beaver" in a row, I began to feel restless. I pulled up the on-screen menu and searched for ESPN, a network I don't believe I had willingly watched in my life. In short order, I remembered why. Two hulking former players sat side by side behind a desk. They wore expensive silk suits and perfectly knotted ties in bold colors. One wore trendy glasses and the other had perfectly styled hair. They were nice to look at, but tedious to listen to. The clichés fell as fast as last night's snow: *They're going to have to give one hundred and ten percent today, Bill; It's ice, ice, baby for returning Stanley Cup champ, Dale Somethingoranother; If they want to win this game, they're going to have to score more goals than the other team;* and on and on. I was just about to rejoin the Beave, when the camera found the home team skating onto the ice. Instinctively, I leaned in, peering at each indistinguishable player as he skated out. I realized I didn't know Josh's number.

"And, this is the last home stand for the Showboats until after the holidays," one of the preened anchors announced.

"Looks like the crowd is down a little today, Bill," the other, named Ted, surmised as the camera panned the blue seats, section after section. "Lots of fans watching from the comfort of home today."

"Six inches of snow fell over St. Louis last night, folks," Bill filled in for those not living in the area. "Did you have any trouble getting here?"

"No, Bill, I didn't. Downtown's pretty clear. So, if you're looking for some fun this afternoon, come on down to Arch Arena for a—"

"Sweet time when the Showboats put it to the Oilers. It'll be the icing on your cake!"

"Tickets available at the door," Bill added, sounding suspiciously like the voice at the end of the cutlery infomercial which makes the "special offer" to the first thirty-five callers.

I blame the sugar and caffeine. I blame Thomas Kincaid. I blame Nanna and her red Land Rover. I blame the makers of unending supplies of white underwear. I showered. I put on perfume, for heaven's sake. I put one of the two colored bras I own—a dusky purple satin one I bought as a Valentine's gift to myself the year before—and a bright blue sweater. I stuffed Josh's business card in my pocket along with two twenty-dollar bills and I drove downtown. There was a moment when

I hesitated, money in hand as a cute, little smiling twenty-something asked, "How many?" and I nearly walked away. The crisp bill had become soggy from the nervous perspiration in my palm. I couldn't speak. There was a loud buzzer sounding somewhere inside the arena and the crowd, however small Bill and Ted had made it out to be, cheered as one.

"Miss Smythe?" The incredulity in the familiar voice was vaguely irritating. I had as much right to be here as anyone else. I turned. "Miss Smythe, hi."

It was Abel Northshore. "Are you here for the game?" He was flabbergasted.

"Yeah." I nodded and forced a smile.

"Yeah?" He raised his eyebrows and looked at me as if I had cursed at him. I don't permit my students to use that word in class. It's "Yes" or "Of course," never "Yeah."

"Yeah," I repeated, trying to make light, and leaned in conspiratorially. "It's a snow day. Yeah?"

"Yeah." He broke into a relieved smile. "I didn't know you liked hockey."

"I don't," I said without thinking.

He was confused. I was confused. The twenty–something waiting for my money was confused.

"Two, ma'am?" She tried to regain my attention as two or three more people lined up behind me.

"She's with me," Abel said, waving to the girl behind the window.

"Okay, Abe." She winked at him.

"Wanna go in?" Abel asked me.

"Sure," I squeaked, discomfort settling in my stomach like last night's pumpkin chili.

Inside, the ice rink had the most peculiar smell. Having been raised in a smaller Midwestern town, I hadn't had much opportunity to be exposed to hockey growing up. In fact, until I took the position in St. Louis, I hadn't realized how truly dedicated fans of the game are. On the highway between downtown and the suburbs, bumper stickers looking like bandages stained bright blue pose the profound question, DO YOU BLEED BLUE?, and oversized magnets shaped like the trademarked Showboat Wheel cling to car doors. I had lived full-time in the area for five years and still had not attended a game. Following Abel up to the seats, I paused to look behind me. Down below, grown men dressed as hulking snowmen raced up and down the ice. The patterns they followed were irregular and random, it seemed to me. The colors were a blur. The panoramic view was not unlike looking into a gigantic kaleidoscope.

"Miss Smythe, we're here," Abel called from a few steps up.

I looked to see who *we* were and saw only Abel and another young man whose face I recognized from the halls at school. Some snow day.

I sat beside him. Abel was as uncomfortable as I was, but after a gentlemanly attempt at introductions—"Miss Smythe, this is Kyle. This is my English teacher"—the two adolescents were engrossed in the action. I settled into my molded chair and tried to decipher the hieroglyphics of masculine competitiveness and the rules of the game. I came to the following conclusions:

1. The team wearing blue is our team. Duh.
2. The guys squatting down at the ends try to keep the puck from going in the nets.
3. If you do something wrong and get caught at it, you get to sit down for a couple of minutes in a little glass box.
4. The fan favorite insult is, "You suck!"

Sitting next to Abel and Kyle—who both seemed to tremendously enjoy yelling, "You suck!"—I felt rather embarrassed by the intensity of their jeers, but dismissed my discomfort so that I could avoid moving to another part of the arena and sitting alone.

A loud buzzer sounded and the crowd went wild. Abel and Kyle leaped to their feet and knocked their fists together and grunted. I stood too, thinking it might be time for the seventh inning stretch, a custom I was familiar with and heartily approved of. When no one started singing, though, I looked at Abel and Abel looked at me.

"So, is that it?" I asked, forcing a smile.

"Game?" he asked incredulously.

"Yeah."

"There's still a period left. Haven't you been to a hockey game before?" he asked as Kyle pushed past mumbling something about nachos.

"Actually, I haven't."

"No way!"

"Nope." I shrugged. "This is my first hockey game."

Abel sat, reeling from the revelation and repeating "No way" to himself as if saying it would make it so.

"So"—I sat beside him—"how many periods are there?"

"Three."

"That means no halftime, then," I attempted as a joke.

"No," he answered very seriously. "There are twenty minutes between periods. Look, I could get you something if you want. Nachos? Coke?"

"Oh, no thank you." I suddenly felt very uncomfortable.

"It's okay, it's free." He really wanted an excuse to get away for a minute. "I'm the captain's brother. They know me here," he added with a grin.

"Well, in that case"—I punched his arm playfully—"a Coke would be great."

"I'll be right back." The sudden release of tension around his mouth was painfully obvious to me.

I felt a slight sense of relief too, as I was left alone with thousands of others. I had always enjoyed the feeling of being alone in a crowd. The sound was deafening in the arena, a consistent and unrelenting roar, like having a seashell attached to your ear permanently. There was a lot of motion, but too many people for anyone to be distinguishable. I realized that the odds of someone looking directly at me and seeing me were very slim. I was pleasantly invisible. I played a game with myself, trying to focus on a single face in the crowd opposite me. I squinted and strained. My imagination filled in a great many details: A woman wearing a pink sweat suit and a yellow stocking cap, a large man with a Santa beard and a red nose, a young couple mouthing the words, "I love you," over and over again.

The clock was down to five minutes and Abel still hadn't returned. I was beginning to wonder if I'd been stood up when an usher appeared at my side with a note. I was perplexed. No one knew I was here, so this couldn't be word of an emergency and, as mannerly as he had been, I couldn't see Abel sending word to my seat of his unexpected departure. I thanked the beaming girl and wondered as she clumped away in her heavy-soled shoes if a tip would have been appropriate. I opened the note and read.

Patricia,

Abel told me you were here. I hope you are bringing me good news. I would like to take you to dinner after the game to discuss the details of our arrangement (or, if necessary, to entice you further). Please wait for me. Enjoy the game!

Josh

My face burned the same way it had burned that day in seventh grade when Nathan Peterson had unexpectedly taken my hand on the way to social studies class.

Abel arrived with a monstrous plastic cup filled to the brim with crushed ice and soda. A whole day's worth of calories, I thought, thanking him and taking a long draw on the straw, hoping the cold liquid would help cool my visage.

"So, which one is your brother?" I asked as the players returned to the ice.

"Number twenty-two," Abel said, pointing. "Right wing."

"What's that mean? Right wing?"

"It's his position. He starts to the right of the center. They use him on the power play a lot."

"What's a power play?"

A buzzer sounded and the teams met at the middle of the rink. Abel's eyes quickly returned to the ice, anticipation showing in his face. The learning moment had passed.

"Time for face-off," he said, distracted now. "I'll show you a power play when we get one. Okay?"

"Okay." I grinned. It was kind of fun seeing this kid who spent the whole semester making every effort to convince me that he was incapable of doing his work take me in hand to teach me something. He got to be the expert today and I felt good about that.

I sat back and drank my soda, applauding politely whenever the crowd cheered. When there were about eight minutes left in the game, Abel leaned over close.

"Okay, you see how they just sent number twelve from the other team into the box?"—he kept his eyes forward, directing my attention appropriately—"When you have a guy in the box, your team is shorthanded. You have one less player than the other team. That means that the other team, us, is on the power play. Twelve got two minutes for roughing . . ."

I nearly choked. "Roughing? The whole game looks like roughing to me."

Abel smiled indulgently. "Yeah. Well, he got two minutes in the box and so we're on the power play. We should have a better chance to score for two minutes."

"Where's your brother?"

"There," he pointed.

I watched for two minutes without taking my eyes off number twenty-two. He was graceful, beautiful in his execution. To focus strictly on him was meditation, a spiritual high. The control he retained over body, stick, and puck was fluid, poetic. When, with five seconds to go, he reached out and captured control of the puck, brought his arms up and swung, there was a hush in the crowd and the collective will of the fans seemed to force the goal. Before there was time to blink, everyone in the arena, myself included, jumped in the air and let loose with his or her own variation on "Yippee!"

"All right!" Kyle yelled and slapped Abel on the shoulder.

"Yes!" Abel kept saying and punched Kyle in the arm.

"That's it!" I heard myself scream and spilled Coke on my foot.

But the celebration was short-lived. The exuberant

crowd suddenly began booing and I noted the serious look on Abel's face. On the ice, one of the refs and Josh were facing each other down.

"Goal!" Kyle shouted.

"Let it stand!" Abel yelled.

"What's going on?" I whispered by his ear.

"The ref called charging," Abel said with disgust. "No goal."

Though I hadn't a clue what charging meant and couldn't fathom why the shot wouldn't count when I had seen the puck go into the net with my own eyes, I didn't think it was the time to further my education. The crowd had gotten ugly.

I sat back in my seat and nursed my soda. Josh was sent to the box for two minutes and the last five minutes of the game were agonizing. The score, which had been close throughout the game, went in favor of the other team and those who bleed blue had taken their beating.

"Wow," I said when it was all over. "That's some game. Do you play too?" I asked Abel.

"Nah, I just like to watch."

"Well, thanks for explaining the power play to me. And for the Coke too."

"You're welcome." Abel blushed.

Kyle pushed past. "See ya, man."

"Nice to meet you," I called after him.

"So," I said when he sat down again.

"So."

"Has your brother told you about his idea?" I began tentatively.

"Yeah," he said without looking at me. I was starting to regret I had let myself assume such casual use of language with him.

"What do you think?"

He shrugged. "What do *you* think?"

"I don't know," I said honestly. "It's an interesting offer. Very interesting."

He braved a look up. "You think so?"

"Not something that comes along every day."

"They're not bad. Road trips, I mean."

"I'm sure not." I sucked up the last straw-rattling remains of soda. He didn't say anything more. "What are your plans after high school?" I asked, relying on the old standby of teacher-student conversation.

"Don't know yet."

"That's okay, I didn't know what I wanted to do when I was your age either. Sometimes, I still don't know what I want to do."

He snorted as if he understood the irony of it all. "Yeah."

"Well, I'm thinking about it."

"Really?" He seemed to brighten.

"You should know that your brother promised me you'd be angelic." I nudged him. Abel didn't react at all and I thought I sensed a darker mood falling over him, much like the brooding I'd noted in his countenance so many times before in class. "I don't expect you to be angelic," I whispered. "Just do the right thing, that's all."

He nodded. We sat in strained silence for what seemed an eternity, but in reality was only a matter of seconds before a long shadow covered my lap. I looked up to see Josh, blue eyes, broad chest, and wet curls towering over me. Abel looked up too.

"Good game," he said.

"Thanks," Josh reached behind me and punched his brother on the shoulder. "Did you really watch, or did you spend all your time talking Stacy out of free food?" he joked.

"Oh, he watched." I came quickly to Abel's defense. "He taught me all about the power play."

"Taught?" Josh sat down on the stair next to me.

"She's never been to a game before." Abel leaned across me, speaking in hushed tones as if the fact was an embarrassment.

"No way." Josh looked at me to confirm the truth of what his brother was saying.

I laughed suddenly at the absurdity of their awe and the striking similarity of their unrehearsed responses.

"That's what I said, no way."

"It's true." I forced myself to stop the now nervous giggling that had crept into my voice and threatened to undo me. "Where I grew up—no hockey. Little town way down near the bootheel."

"Incredible," Josh said. "I guess when something is so much a part of your own life you forget it's not that way for everyone." He seemed lost in thought. "Abe, you headed home?"

"Yeah." Abel stood. "I have some English to do." He cast a sidelong glance in my direction. "*Canterbury Tales.* Yuck."

"Hey," I said, "it's bawdy stuff, you know. Be sure to read the footnotes. You'll see what I mean."

"Drive carefully," Josh said as Abel took the twenty he'd been offered. "Order a pizza if you want. I won't be too late." He amended his promise in hushed tones and Abel nodded before excusing himself. Josh turned back to me. "So, what do you like?"

"Don't you want to know if we're in the celebration or bargaining mode?" I asked, teasing.

"I thought I'd let it unfold over dinner."

"Oh. Well, in that case, I like . . ." My mind raced. Every answer I could truthfully give sounded boring and staid. I like steak and burgers, Mexican and Chinese. I like pasta and pizza and all the other Americanized fare you can find at the exit ramps along I-44. My brain locked. All I could think of was pumpkin chili. *Nanna. What would Nanna say?* "I like Ethiopian and Thai," I said it with as much sincerity as I could muster. Outside of peanut sauce I didn't know what Thai food really consisted of. And as for Ethiopian? No clue.

"Ethiopian and Thai," he repeated, his mouth screwed up tightly. Was he in pain or just thinking? "I think there's a place on the Loop. Do you know it?"

"Beads in the window?" I invented a detail which sounded authentic to me.

"Yeah." Josh snapped his fingers. "All right. Let's go." He stood and offered his hand.

I placed my cold fingers lightly in his palm as I stood. He closed his hand around mine. "You're cold," he noted.

"It's an ice rink." I grinned.

"You'll have to wear gloves next time."

Next time. Next time? Will there be a next time?

"What did you think of the game?" he asked as we reached the top and headed for the exit.

"Good night, Josh," another cute young worker, this one with a shock of neon-blue hair, called.

"Good night." He waved.

"It was okay." I tried to sound nonchalant.

"Okay?"

"It was good."

"Good." He turned the word over in his mouth, exploring it for layers of meaning. Discovering none, he said, "Well, I'm glad it was good."

Josh drove a 1968 powder-blue Mustang with red pin striping. I swear, it's true. Glass-packed muffler, tinted windows, dual exhaust. I slid into the navy-blue vinyl bucket seat and knocked my knee on the gear shift. A set of dog tags hung around the mirror, but it was too dark to read what they said. They clinked together when he climbed in and started it up.

"Fun car," I remarked. "Not what I would have expected of a national league hockey player."

"Cool is cool, no matter what year it is." He smiled and revved the engine playfully.

I laughed in spite of myself. "A boy on my block had one of these. It wasn't too cool. It was pea-green with one orange door and a torn vinyl top."

"Shameful," Josh said, shaking his head. "Don't you think it's shameful when people don't recognize a true classic?"

"Oh, I do," I teased.

He glanced my way and smiled. "You look good in it," he said.

"Pardon?"

"In the car, the classic. You look good in it."

"Thanks," I said, not certain I understood the compliment.

"Not everyone can carry it off. Some women are too"—he thought for a moment, drumming his fingers on the large steering wheel—"they're too uptight, or full of themselves to just enjoy the ride." He hesitated. "No pun intended."

I smirked.

"So, *Canterbury Tales*, huh?"

"Yes," I said, slipping out of my snow day recklessness and resuming proper language usage.

"I haven't read that in years," he mused. "I remember the *Nun's Priest's Tale* and the *Wife of Bath*, but that's about it."

"I'm impressed you remember any of your Chaucer. He's not a great asset on the ice, is he?"

"No, not really." He swung into a metered lot at the head of the Loop. "I do find use for a few good Shakespearean insults now and again, though."

"Your old English teachers would be proud."

"Hey, you are talking to a BA in romantic literature, thank you very much."

"Really?" I was truly astonished. I would have guessed he had majored in physical fitness or recreation.

"Really. Are you impressed?"

"I am."

The sun had gone down and the shops were alight with strings of racing red and green pinpoints. I watched Josh feed several quarters into the meter and wondered how long he planned to linger over dinner.

"I thought we might want to walk a bit afterward," he said as if he had read my mind.

He offered his arm and I took it gratefully. Why hadn't I thought to put some gloves in my bag? Standing this close to the professional athlete, I could smell the intoxicating combination of his leather coat and soap. I breathed it in eagerly. Despite the cold evening, I felt warm, so the shiver that overtook me caught me off guard and Josh drew me closer to him, putting his arm around my shoulders. I snuggled in against my own better judgment. "Thank you," I whispered.

We walked to the place our imaginations had contrived and found two real possibilities: A Lebanese restaurant with "garlic" in its name, and an abandoned storefront with nothing left but a row of beads in the window.

"That must have been it," Josh surmised.

"Must have been."

"Anything else along the way look good to you?"

"Well, there's Blueberry Hill back there," I said hopefully. The thought of a big, juicy burger was very appealing right now. The cookies had long since left me.

"Kind of noisy," he said.

"True."

"What about that?" Josh pointed across the road. "Looks quiet."

"Okay," I said without considering further.

The little restaurant which specialized in fondue was quaint. We were seated at a table by the front window and the blue string of lights which outlined the glass cast a soft, pleasant glow. It was subtly festive. Charming. Peaceful. We ordered white wine and started with crudités and bread cubes with a smoky cheese sauce. The aroma was pungent, but pleasingly warm and earthy. Quiet conversations swirled around us, mingling harmoniously with the soft music overhead. Our own voices seemed to bounce back to us, so protected were we in our public privacy. Here was a feast for the senses. I was aware of the texture of a woven cloth under my fingertips, the warmth of the candle on the back of my hand. When our forks tapped over the steaming bowl, I swear I felt the vibration in my soul. It was a rare and exquisite hour.

"How much do you know about Abel? On a personal level, I mean?" Josh asked as the waitress cleared away our first course.

"I know about his mother. Well, your mother, too, I'm assuming." I felt suddenly awkward discussing familial matters with him. "About her hospitalization." I stopped without further comment.

Abel had written his first essay this year about his mother. It was titled, Something Wicked This Way Comes. It was impassioned and real, gritty and base. I remember being startled that a young man who didn't really know me well enough to trust me at that point in time would choose to share such personal information. The story went something like this: Mrs. Northshore, widowed at the young age of thirty-five and left with two boys to raise—one a rambunctious fifteen-year-old and the other yet unborn—struggled to maintain a semblance of sanity throughout her youngest son's formative years. There were periods of extended absence when, as Abel was told, the mother was away at a health center recovering from this or that indistinct ailment. During those weeks and months, Josh, the proverbial first-born, cared for Abel under the watchful eye of an auntie whose revolving door romances and constant drinking overshadowed any maternal instinct she might have felt for her nephews. Against the odds, Josh had pursued hockey with a drive unknown and incomprehensible to Abel, who was content to sit in the stands and watch. When Josh went away to college, Abel was left to fend for himself, except on holidays when, gratefully, his older brother would come home and make everything wonderful for those few weeks. Then, Josh would return to school and Abel was left alone again. Somewhere around his thirteenth birthday, Abel's mother suddenly worsened, less and less able to control her emotional outbursts and, seemingly, less and less willing to seek or accept help for herself. Ultimately, on the occasion of Abel's sixteenth birthday, she was committed to the state's care and Abel was placed under the permanent guardianship of his older brother, now an NHL star.

There were details aplenty, too disturbing and sad to recount. Under the softly pulsing glow of the blue Christmas lights, tears threatened. I looked intently at the backs of my hands and hoped Josh would not feel it necessary to fill me in further.

"He's had a rough time," was all he said. It was understated and yet, enough.

"I'm sorry."

"Anyway." He tried to shake off the mood as a second course was set before us.

By the time the pot of rich chocolate and plate of fruit and cake were placed in front of us, silence seemed to have settled in for the night. I was uncomfortable and mentally trying out ways to couch my refusal of his offer in inoffensive terms. Whatever inclination I might have felt earlier in the day to go for it, as my grandmother would say, had passed. Probably, it was just the exhilaration of considering something out of the ordinary; a strong desire to break routine. Or, it could have been desire of another kind; I'm not so self-evasive as to deny it. I found the contemplation of Josh Northshore quite pleasurable. But, there is a line of demarcation which must be protected between profession and person. It seemed all too blurry at this point in time.

"So, what do you think?" he asked softly as he bit through a chocolate-drenched square of angel food cake. The sight of his mouth working over the sweets nearly undid me.

"About Abel and Christmas," I began slowly. "I think it's really wonderful that you went to all this trouble for him."

"Uh oh," he whispered.

"I'm sorry, it's just that I don't see how I can possibly do this and remain"—what was it I was trying to say?—"professionally detached."

"Detached? Since when are teachers detached?"

"Too strong a word. Unbiased."

"Better. Thank you for at least considering it."

He was genuine. He meant it. I believed that he had held out no real hope that I would agree; that the decision had truly been mine to make and he would not have tried to exert any pressure on me.

"What will happen?" he asked as he traced trails in a puddle of chocolate with the end of a strawberry; they opened ahead of it and closed behind it. It was mesmerizing to watch, like tracing his path across the ice on the power play.

"Happen?"

"To Abel. He'll be down a half-credit after Christmas. It's his senior year."

"Have you talked to anyone in the counseling center? It could be that he has enough credits without this half."

Josh didn't answer, only shook his head. There was no chance.

"I'm sorry," I whispered, feeling ashamed of myself and not really understanding why.

Teaching high school is like walking a tightrope. You want students to be accountable, to accept responsibility for their own decisions and to suffer consequences for the bad ones while they're still in a relatively safe environment. At the same time, you don't want to condemn a kid for making a few mistakes along the way. You have to be fair and consistent, yet need to consider individual circumstances. Abel Northshore was one of about ten I could name whose graduations would be iffy come May. It was a pattern with him. A student doesn't get to the senior year with a perfect track record and then have it all fall apart. There are signs along the way. There are helps along the way. I've said many times, and firmly believe, that a kid in the public schools these days has to purposely try to fail.

Questions might be asked if I accepted pay for tutoring my own student off the clock. Certainly, eyebrows would be raised. While I was sure any doubts could be allayed by one perusal of the district's board policies and any backlash would be minor and easily remedied,

I disliked the idea of compromising my professional stance. Still, looking across the table at this troubled older brother and legal guardian, I wondered if being fair and consistent was good enough for me this time. If digging my heels in against potential whispers or remarks was reason enough to ignore an opportunity to really make a difference for someone.

Josh paid the bill and we left the comfortable warmth of the restaurant. "Are you up for a stroll?" he asked hopefully, turning up the collar of his coat against the chilly breeze. "I'll loan you my gloves."

"Sure," I said, sliding my hands deep inside the fleecy warmth. "Thanks."

Josh offered me his arm to keep me steady on the potentially slick sidewalks. We walked that way like old friends or new lovers. We passed a used book shop, pausing to look in on a poetry reading. Josh stopped to admire a dirt bike in a window, wondering aloud if Abel would like to have one.

"I worry about him," he offered. "He doesn't seem to have any interests of his own."

I didn't know what to say, so I said nothing. A handful of carolers from Washington U's choral music department had gathered on a street corner to spread Christmas cheer and we lingered just long enough to join in a sing-along of "Deck the Halls" and "Winter Wonderland" before heading back to Arch Arena where my frozen car sat wondering what had become of me.

"Thank you for the evening," I said as I leaned back

into the Mustang. "I enjoyed myself very much and I'm sorry I wasn't able to give you the answer you were hoping for."

"Win some, lose some." He smiled, disappointment evident in his eyes.

"I'll be in touch after the break. We'll think about what needs to happen for Abel. Okay?"

"That would be great."

I closed the door. The gentleman Northshore waited until I had locked myself in and my windows had defrosted before he let me out ahead of him and we parted ways at the street. I felt happy and sad all at once. Like I had hauled up a treasure from the deep and promptly thrown it overboard. I felt wistful and suddenly very alone.

My house was dark as I pulled into the drive. My untrained impulsiveness had taken me out at midday without thought to the fact that it would be dark when I came home. The streets were clear and there would be school tomorrow. I hurried inside and slipped out of my clothes, tossing the dusky purple brassiere back into the never-open-this-drawer drawer and pulled on my favorite flannel nightgown and thick bed socks. Snuggling in for the night, I shut off the lamp and went to sleep.

I dreamed of giant fondue pots transformed into ice rinks where miniaturized Joshes and Abels skated around and around under my watchful eye while carolers sang fa-la-la faster and faster and a woman concealed by shadows poked her stainless steel fingers through her cage and knocked the Northshore brothers over. Then it all started again like some sick wind-up toy.

When I woke at six o'clock the next morning, I grabbed my jeans from the heap of laundry on the floor and fished out the business card I had kept within arm's reach since two days before. I picked up the phone and dialed.

Chapter Three

"**I** changed my mind," I said as soon as he answered.

"Hello?" His voice was garbled with sleepiness.

"It's Patricia. Patricia Smythe. I've changed my mind. I'll go along and help Abel earn his credit."

He snapped to suddenly. "Are you sure?"

"Yes," I said forcefully, still trying to convince myself that it was the right thing.

"Well, all right! Thank you. I mean, really, thank you."

"So, when do we leave and what do I need to take?"

"I'll e-mail you the itinerary tomorrow when we get the final copy. Casual stuff mainly, but you might want to bring a dress for restaurants. Don't forget your gloves," he teased. "We need to be at the airport at four-thirty A.M. Tuesday. Abe and I will pick you up so you don't have to leave your car at the airport."

"I don't want to be any trouble," I protested. "I'll have my grandmother drop me off."

"That's fine. Well, if you have any questions, be sure to call me back. And thanks again. It means the world. Really."

I hung up the phone and dressed for school. My brain was buzzing with anticipation. I called Nanna during my conference period and asked her to meet me for dinner. I had a favor to ask.

The day inched by. Fifth period seemed remarkably calm and I was alert enough to at least consider the possibility that the less interest I showed in them the better off I might be. Other classes, like the last one of the day, a group of seniors including Abel Northshore seemed almost needy. Overall, they were afraid to commit anything to paper until they knew exactly what they wanted to say. They allowed no room for revision or reconsideration. They expected perfection the first time. This drove me crazy; however, I couldn't fault them because I am much the same way. Mistakes are messy and I prefer neat. Better to hang back and let things develop before committing yourself to a course of action. At least, that's how I live. Nanna says that if I haven't yet, I certainly will miss out on the opportunity of a lifetime that way. Caution is for the coward, she says.

"You are kidding me." Nanna nearly dropped her glass. She fumbled it and finally brought it firmly down on the tabletop.

People were turning to stare. "It's not that big a deal," I leaned forward and whispered harshly.

"Not that big a deal? This is huge! This is . . . what? What is it? So unlike you. So . . ."

"Frivolous?"

"No."

"Irresponsible?"

"No."

"Brave?" I held my breath. Brave is the last word my grandmother would ever have used to describe me.

"That's it!" she said, fists balled up like a boxer. "Brave. Good girl. It's about time too. Now, the first thing we have to do is to go lingerie shopping."

I nearly choked. "What?"

"Lingerie shopping. You'll need some new under-things."

"Nanna, I am going on this trip as a professional educator. It's not a tryst of some sort."

"I know that darling." She patted my hand in that annoyingly patronizing manner she has. "But if Mr. Northshore suggested you might bring along a dress for restaurants, then I suggest the gentleman is thinking that your professional day job will actually end at the end of the day and he is hoping, somewhat presumptuously perhaps, but hoping nonetheless, that he might have the pleasure of your company for dinners, dancing . . ." She left the thought hanging there for the imagination.

"Nanna," I protested, "Josh may have the pleasure of

my company for dinner. He may even have the pleasure of my company for dancing, but that in no way implies a need for new lingerie." I took a long swallow of the ice water before me. My face had warmed and my hands felt shaky.

"Of course it does, Patricia."

"No, Nanna, it doesn't."

"Dearest"—she leaned across the table and beckoned me closer with her bony fingers and shocking pink nails—"I don't mean to sound insulting, but if you are going to be dining with professional athletes in restaurants which require more than casual wear, you will need a dress."

"I have dresses."

"A dress fit for the occasion?" She raised her eyebrows.

She was right. My dresses bordered on the matronly. Plenty of earth tones in tea-lengths, shawl collars and covered buttons.

"A dress like the little cocktail job I still have which seems to be back in style? I kept it because it was my favorite and because I was wearing it the night I danced with Pat Boone."

"What?"

"Never mind. The point is it is emerald-green, figure-hugging and very, very feminine. It will look great on you, but"—she motioned me closer still—"it won't look right at all if you wear it over one of those industrial-strength brassieres of yours. So"—she sat back and lifted her glass—"lingerie shopping. Top of the list."

I sat back, bewildered, but willing to acquiesce to her expertise.

Josh e-mailed the itinerary as promised. The trip looked like a whirlwind to me. We would leave St. Louis early Tuesday morning for a game in Toronto that night. Over the next couple of weeks, they would play in Seattle, staying there for New Year's Eve, and finally end up in Chicago before arriving back in St. Louis the day before school was to reconvene. Between games there were practices and dinners, signings and a variety of other events. Most intriguing to me was the item on December 25 at 7 p.m. It read SANTA BABY. That was it. My mind raced, but the only ideas I could come up with were lurid possibilities based on the cheesecakey renditions of the old song by the same name. I thought it best to leave the unknown unknown.

There were hotels listed at each stop and a second page which had no meaning to me whatsoever: A listing of team standings. At the very bottom of the itinerary was a postscript:

Patricia,

Thank you again for being willing to do this for us. I appreciate it more than you could possibly know. Please call if you have any questions about

*the itinerary or if you decide you'd like a ride to
the airport.*

> *In your debt,*
> *Josh*

The last few days of school flew by. My American
Lit classes finished reading *The Adventures of Huckle-
berry Finn,* one of my favorites, and we spent the last
two class periods before the break collecting research
for the project that would begin when we returned.
My seniors trudged through the last of Dante's *Inferno,*
which seemed strangely appropriate as we entered into
the season of "senioritis" and they began dropping like
flies until only a handful were actually present on the
last day.

About the trip, I was giddy. My early reservations
had given way to out and out excitement. It had been a
long time since I had stepped off the treadmill of work
to home to weekend to work to home to weekend. In
my state of distraction, I had actually forgotten to con-
sult my secret Grecian holiday calendar under my blotter. The last day marked off was December 15, the day
Josh Northshore had walked into my life.

Walked into my life. There's a thought. Is that really
what had happened? Physically, yes. He had turned up
on my doorstep, so to speak, and had imposed himself
in such a way that I hadn't really been away from him
since. He and his offer had taken over my thinking since
that very moment. I had gone about my days in a swirl

of masculine imagery, athleticism, and holiday fantasia, forgetting the things that usually seemed so important to me. I hadn't seen a news update in a week. Hadn't made a new grocery list. Hadn't sent out Christmas cards and hadn't RSVPed to Virginia Calhoun's annual New Year's Eve bash.

Let them wonder, I thought devilishly, delighting in the idea that I, Patricia Smythe, had a secret rendezvous for the holidays.

The day before we were to leave, I met Nanna at the mall. She was festive in green and gold corduroy overalls and red suede ankle boots. I laughed when I saw her.

"Are you lost? Shouldn't you be helping the kids into Santa's lap?" I teased.

"I've been looking for a second job," she quipped. "Can I buy you a pretzel? A little fortification before shopping?"

"Sure." The recent disruption to my routines had also disrupted my usually semi-healthy diet. I had eaten more peanut butter sandwiches lately than I cared to admit. I wanted to have my grading caught up before I left so I could concentrate on Abel's work over the break.

The mall was abuzz with shoppers merrily chatting as they went about their business, oversized shopping bags stuffed to bursting bumping against their legs as they wove their way through the crowds. Tinny sounding tunes piped through speakers mingled with the hubbub, making spirits bright. The Santa I had noted before was on a throne and children lined up as far as I could see to wait their turn to climb the lushly carpeted stairs and be lifted into the lap of luxury. Even as I watched, a little girl dressed in purple velveteen and with golden curls bouncing like Slinkies, flew up off her feet, pink tulle petticoats flashing innocently before she was lowered, light as a feather, onto the jolly man's welcoming knees and into his warm embrace. He leaned in, giving her his complete attention, nodding politely and throwing his head back in a vibrant laugh. She giggled too. They were the picture of Christmas. I was caught by the sight of them. Nanna was too.

"Isn't she sweet?"

"She's adorable."

"You used to look like that. Nellie Olsen curls, I called them." She took a bite of her warm, sugar-and-cinnamon-coated pretzel.

"I always hated that. Who wants to be compared to Nellie Olsen?" I reasoned. "Mom always called them sausage curls." I smiled, a warm memory flickering through my mind. "She used to roll them up for me on Saturday nights. I felt so elegant with my hair done up that way."

"You looked prissy," Nanna said bluntly. Speaking her mind was never a problem for the matriarch.

"Thanks," I bristled and quickly bit into my snack to avoid provocation.

"I have a picture of you on Santa's lap somewhere," she continued without catching the hint of ire in my voice.

My grandmother and my mother had been at odds for most of my life. My mother was a very practical person, quiet and proud. Nanna had failed to see the value of such a subdued life and had pushed and pushed her daughter to be a part of things—go to parties, go to dances, take things less seriously, live a little. Instead, my mother, in her own sort of rebellion, had retreated further and further away from her own mother and into herself. That I was born out of wedlock was almost reason to rejoice for Nanna. It meant that her daughter, Cynthia Louise, had finally done something which, at that time at least, was still on most people's no-no list.

Mother confided to me many years later that it was her desperate need to be accepted for who she was that had led her into the embrace of a man I never met and never cared to meet, my father. He had been bookish, like herself, the polar opposite of the boys her mother had arranged dates with for her throughout her adolescence—miserable boys who, once they realized how genuinely shy she was, never bothered to ask her again. They had found mutual pleasure in the study of the poetry of the romantic era under the tutelage of a common professor at the university. They had picnicked together, visited museums, and enjoyed the opera together. It seemed natural. It seemed right, she said. When reality crashed their private party, she found herself pregnant and alone. He returned to the arms of the wife he had never mentioned before. She was ashamed, scorned, afraid. My grandmother was there, but not with the comfort she needed. They raised me together and so I learned by experiencing the extremes of the socialization process. Mother never dated again, to my knowledge, and when I was nineteen, just entering my sophomore year at Mizzou, she was killed. A car driven by an artist on the way to the gallery where his work was being shown that evening crossed the median and hit her head-on. He was running late. She was, as always, on time and on her way to meet me for dinner. She never arrived and I stayed away from the dorm that night, afraid to go back and receive the bad news, the harbinger of which had already pierced my heart when she wasn't there five minutes ahead of our scheduled meeting time.

My grandmother saw me through the rest of my undergraduate studies and into graduate school. I considered, at her prompting, moving away to another part of the country to really start fresh. She was worried that I had let the trauma of my mother's death adversely affect me and that I was, in her words, becoming too withdrawn, too much like my mother. I opted to stay in my home state. The trip I was planning to Greece was the bravest thing I had done—even though it was still in the planning phase—until I said yes to Josh and to his brother, Abel.

Pretzels gone and sodas slurped up, we ventured into the throng. I stopped at the windows of boutiques specializing in women's career clothing, pointing out sweaters and skirts in rich jewel tones along the way. Nanna pulled me on toward our destination: Lydia's Little Luxuries and

Lingerie, a shop whose trademarks were its purple and green argyle wallpaper and their nearly naked mannequins. I had been in a few times before. They have a great selection of scented lotions. My favorite is Classic Vanilla. I always felt conspicuous leaving that store and toting the garish little shopping bag with its black tissue paper sticking out the of top. I could just see myself running into one of my students. A girl wondering what Miss Smythe bought at Lydia's. Or, worse yet, a gang of boys wondering what Miss Smythe bought at Lydia's.

My palms began to sweat as we entered the shop and Nanna immediately waved over one of the clerks, clad in a black smock clipped at the neck with a purple and green brooch.

"May I help you?" the woman, older than myself and younger than Nanna, asked, sizing us up as she approached.

"My granddaughter here needs a little help with some lingerie."

"I see," she answered, looking me up and down.

"Yes, Roberta"—I read her name tag as I determined to take over the conversation—"I need some help selecting an appropriate piece for a certain dress. Nanna," I said quietly, "I need some Classic Vanilla lotion. Would you go find a bottle for me, please?" I pressed her arm.

"Classic Vanilla?" She was astonished. "Patricia, that's for old women. Why don't we try something new?"

"Fine. You go smell everything they've got. Choose three and I'll pick one. Okay?" I was losing patience.

She was off on her mission. Roberta stood gawking. "The dress is emerald green. It is velvet and fits rather snugly."

"What is the neckline?" Roberta assumed a professional stance.

"It scoops fairly low." I drew a line across my chest at about the right depth.

"Hmm. You look to me about a thirty-six-B. Is that right?"

"Yes." I was impressed.

"Perhaps something in a push-up?" she speculated as she led the way into the treasure trove of feminine luxuries that was the back half of the shop.

"Oh, I don't think a push-up . . ." I never have been particularly comfortable with cleavage.

Roberta turned and shot me a look over her shoulder. She was not a woman to be contradicted. This was her domain. Her specialty. Her area of expertise. If Roberta said push-up then push-up it would be. I tried to imagine how the dress would look with a black lace, gel-enhanced, plunge bra underneath it. I swear color rose to my cheeks.

That's okay, I thought as Roberta took three different designs from the rack and pointed toward the curtained dressing room. *I'll buy it and if I don't like it, I'll wear one of my own.*

Resolved, I entered the dressing room feeling less self-conscious than before. The first was just what I had imagined: Black lace with a front clasp and a rather wide span of nothing across the front. The coverage was spare at the sides and the cool gel inserts pushed up and in, creating a very modern, very seductive-looking cleavage. I turned from front to side and back again, nearly giggling at the change it made in my figure. I reached for the next, a red sateen strapless with cushions where the gel had been in the first one. The effect was much the same. Lastly, a signature purple bra, also lace with a rhinestone ring set at the center. A far cry from my white cotton crisscross. I rather liked this last one and was becoming more and more comfortable with the idea of strutting my stuff. At least for one evening at a fancy restaurant.

"I neglected to mention, madame, that our lingerie is buy two get the third for half price." Roberta's voice carried over the curtain.

"Thank you," I said, feeling suddenly embarrassed and slipping quickly back into my own white cotton.

When I emerged, Nanna was seated outside the door with three bottles of lotion in her arms. "Well?"

I looked to Roberta, whose expression showed sincere doubt about the sale.

"I'll take all three." I handed them to her.

"And the lotions?" She was stunned as she took the lingerie from me.

"Yes, those too."

Nanna surrendered them willingly.

"Could you pick out three pairs of panties to match, please? I wear a size six and prefer French cut." I tried

to sound like a woman familiar with the full range of
styles and who knew precisely what she liked.

"Certainly," she said, a hint of respect now evident in
her tone.

I paid and left with an even larger version of the dis-
tinctive purple and green argyle bag with black tissue
paper peeking from the top. Nanna was speechless. Re-
joining the holiday horde, I forced myself to walk as if I
was carrying a bag of no more interest than if it was
made of brown paper and said BARGAIN BASEMENT on it.

We stopped in another shop or two, Nanna taking
advantage of our trip to purchase a couple of gifts for
friends. As we were heading out the doors and I was
feeling a sense of relief, it happened.

"Miss Smythe."

The boy's voice was familiar. My head buzzed. Was
it Chase? Michael? Joey?

"Miss Smythe?" he repeated, thinking I hadn't heard
him.

I turned. It was Abel Northshore and his friend, Kyle.
"Hello."

"Hi," he said. Kyle stood mute.

"Out shopping?" I asked stupidly.

"Going to the movies."

My right hand started to tremble, the bag of contra-
band becoming suddenly heavy. I kept my eyes locked
with Abel's.

"Miss Smythe," Abel said, suddenly quiet and serious. He stepped toward me. I impulsively moved the

bag around behind me. "Thank you," he said as sheepishly as a child who has been told to be polite.

"For what?"

"For helping me out. I didn't want Josh to ask you in the first place."

"You're welcome. We'll have a good time and get some good work done too. Okay?"

"Sure," he muttered, his ego getting the better of him.

There was an awkward moment in which my grandmother and Kyle seemed to fade into the background and it was only Abel, myself and that awful bag.

"Well, thanks again," he said and stretched out his hand to shake mine.

It was a gesture I had adopted with my students some time ago. Whenever there was controversy in the classroom or some need for me to have less than pleasant dealings with a student, I wanted each one to know that I wasn't holding a grudge. I found it especially helpful in reestablishing good relationships with boys. It wasn't a motherly gesture. It was a sign of mutual respect. It pleased me that Abel initiated it here. I reached out to take his hand and saw his face turn pink. With our right hands clasped, the Little Luxuries bag swung between us like a pendulum. I heard Kyle smother a laugh.

"I'll see you at the airport, then," I said, recovering my voice and withdrawing my hand.

"See you then," Abel said, turning to Kyle and punching him solidly in the arm as the two walked away.

Nanna began to laugh. Not a snigger. Not a chuckle.

A snorting, gasping, rib-gripping, rolling-on-the-floor laugh that lasted until we were on the highway, subsided, and returned intermittently, like the flurries blowing across the windshield.

"Okay, enough," I said when we finally pulled into the drive. "Enough."

We went in and I took the hated shopping bag to my room, setting it next to the suitcase I had begun packing.

Nanna called from the living room, "Want to order a pizza?"

"Sure. Number's on the fridge."

Since I would be gone for Christmas, Nanna and I had contrived to celebrate early. She would stay the night, driving me to the airport in time for that early flight.

"What will you do Christmas Eve?" I asked, savoring the hot pizza and appreciating the flavors that were in stark contrast to the sweet sandwiches, which had been my usual fare of late.

"Mr. O'Malley and I are going to a party."

"Who's Mr. O'Malley?"

"I met him at my dating class," she said, a glint in her eye.

"Someone special?"

"Aren't they all?" She winked.

We exchanged gifts over hot chocolate and sugar cookies before going to bed. I gave her a subscription to *Time of Your Life Magazine,* a publication geared toward active seniors and which often featured cover photos of a granny rock-climbing, or a granddad on a jet ski, or some other bizarre image, and a bottle of Classic Vanilla lotion.

"Well," she said when she opened it, "I am at least the right age for it."

I opened my gifts next. First, a pocket-sized edition of *A Girl's Guide to Hockey.*

"Thanks," I said, flicking through the pages.

"It doesn't hurt to know a thing or two about the man's business." Nanna grinned. "Open your other one."

Under the silver wrapping and the blue bow, the unassuming little box held an absolute treasure: A ruby pendant, square cut and on a thin, silver chain.

"Oh, Nanna!" I gasped, lifting it from the box. "It's beautiful."

"It's an antique," she said, reaching out to help me put it on. "It belonged to my mother. I was never very fond of it. Too plain. Your mother loved it. I promised I'd give it to her on her wedding day, but . . ." She abandoned the unhappy thought and patted my shoulders. "Let me see." I turned and watched as her eyes misted over. "It suits you."

I stood and crossed to a mirror which hung over the piano. It was a beautiful stone. I fingered it gently, tenderly, as if touching my mother's face once again.

"You'll wear it with the green dress, won't you?" Nanna was standing behind me now.

"Of course," I said, my voice choked. "Nanna, thank you. It's perfect."

"Nothing like a hand-me-down Christmas gift, huh?" She tried to make light.

"Nothing at all," I said and hugged her close.

"Well, we have to be up in less than five hours," she announced. "Probably ought to try to get a little shut-eye."

"Yes," I said, still stunned.

"I'll come back by here while you're gone and get everything picked up. We won't mess with it tonight."

We said our good nights and I closed the door to my room. I finished my packing, topping off the heap of winter wear with the newest additions to my personal collection and leaving out what I planned to wear on the flight tomorrow. I checked the alarm three times before dozing off. The light was bright coming through the windows, moon reflecting on snow.

"Merry Christmas, Nanna."

"Merry Christmas, Cynthia."

"Good night."

I didn't correct her. Somewhere inside, I knew she had regrets. I felt a twinge of guilt about spending the holidays away from her but forced myself to concentrate on getting to sleep. I conjured up Josh Northshore's face and fell into a sweet repose.

Chapter Four

My new tube of lip gloss was confiscated at a security check. Thirteen dollars and change, an extravagant impulse buy from a cosmetics counter clerk who promised "kissable plumpness with a hint of sparkle, just right for the holidays," was tossed into a nearby waste can by a man in an official-looking vest and a hat, which shielded his prying eyes from my view as he sorted through my personal effects. He didn't comment. He didn't question. He just sorted and tossed.

"Next," he said, setting my bag on the conveyor belt and waving me past.

Entering the terminal, I spotted the Northshore men. Josh, who stood a head taller than Abel, was conversing with another man of similar stature, a teammate presumably, who was very animated when he spoke. Abel was scrunched up in a corner chair, buds in his ears and nose stuck in a magazine. I noted his backpack in the seat beside him, the same one he carried to class with him—dark gray with tattoo-like drawings in permanent black marker. I smiled. Someone was on the ball, though I wasn't sure which Northshore it was.

Josh looked up and saw me. He waved me across. I walked toward him, nervously but purposefully. I felt my eyes sink in embarrassment as I realized I was the only female in the room.

"Patricia," he began and laid his large hand on my shoulder. "You made it."

"Yes," I said simply and glanced up at him. He was truly beautiful to look at. The morning sun was streaming through the windows overlooking the runway. He glowed in it. Just as he had glowed in the Christmas lights over dinner. Had it already been a week since then?

"Great. Patricia, this is Seth Mitchell."

"How'djado," Seth said and stuck out his lion-sized paw for me to shake. His grip engulfed my hand and nearly dislocated it from the wrist.

"I do fine, thanks," I said through clenched teeth, forcing a smile.

"Seth plays center," Josh said, assuming I knew what that meant. *Note to self, look up the term "center" in the* Girl's Guide.

"Great." I tried to sound impressed.

"Patricia is Abel's English teacher," Josh explained.

"Oh." Seth's eyes widened and he took me in. "You don't look like any English teacher I ever had."

"Seth," Josh said softly.

"No," he continued in his blissful ignorance, "Mrs. Crowe was ancient. She had wiry gray hair she kept pulled back on top of her head and she always wore black orthopedic shoes. You could hear her coming a mile away. Squeak, squeak, squeak."

Sounds straight out of pioneer days," I remarked, hoping this would bring the conversation to a speedy end. Seth was oblivious.

"Yeah," Seth said. "And Mrs. Torkelson was no better. She was a looker, like yourself." He nodded toward me. I smiled and forced a dry chuckle. I got the feeling he really wasn't aware he was saying anything that might be offensive or demeaning. "But the woman had a voice that could crack glass. She was always shouting, 'Boys and girls' "—his voice rose and I noticed Josh glancing around the room—" 'Boys and girls, I want you to commit it to memory. Commit it to memory.' "

"Well, we don't do much memorization these days." I tried to move the conversation along.

"I still remember Mark Anthony's speech in *Julius Caesar.*" He puffed his chest as if he'd just scored a goal or whatever it was he did in hockey. " 'Friends, Romans, countrymen, lend me your ears. I come not to bury Caesar, but to praise him . . . ' "

"That's great," I said as Josh took hold of my elbow

and steered me away from center Seth toward the quiet corner where Abel was seated, now apparently dozing.

"Seth's a great guy but a little loud sometimes."

I laughed out loud. Josh smiled.

"You have a nice laugh," he said.

"Thanks." I was beginning to feel warm and wishing I had chosen a cardigan for the flight instead of a pullover. I tugged at the neck as we moved away from the group.

"So," he said.

"So," I answered.

"Are you ready?"

"I guess so." I shrugged. "This is a little strange but it seems right. You know?"

"I know." He squeezed my arm gently and the warmth in my face grew. "Anything you need, you be sure you let me know. And if Abel gives you any trouble at all . . ."

"You promised he'd be angelic."

"To the best of my ability, I will make sure of it. I guess you'll want to get started when we get to Toronto?"

"Well, actually"—I fished through my handbag for my memo book—"I made out a tentative schedule of what Abel needs to do and how we can best accomplish that in this short amount of time. I thought he might actually get started on some of the reading during this flight so that we can begin discussions and writings and such tomorrow." I retrieved the little notebook from my bag and flipped it open.

"Abe," Josh called. Abel didn't respond. "Excuse

me." He strode across the expanse between himself and his brother.

I watched him go. His shoulders were like those of Atlas, broad, strong. The ivory cable-knit sweater he wore strained across his back and tapered down to meet his waist where my eyes fell immediately to the tantalizing sight of a man in soft blue denim. The scent of him lingered behind, the same scent which had edged my dreams since that night on the Loop: Leather and soap. I felt suddenly dizzy and reached out to steady myself.

Josh shook Abel's shoulder and the younger plucked the tune-carrying speakers out of his ears and looked into his big brother's face. Josh nodded his head in my direction and Abel stood up. They walked toward me and I smiled brightly.

"Hi, Abel," I said. "Ready for all this?"

"Sure," he answered and I found myself smack in the middle of a mall-moment flashback.

"Abe, Miss Smythe would like you to start reading on the plane so that you guys can get right to work when we get to Toronto."

"Okay," Abel answered obediently.

"Did you bring your anthology?" I asked, sounding more like a mother than I meant or wanted to. He nodded. "Start with *Beowulf* on page two-twenty-three. Okay? Be sure to use the footnotes and ask if you have any questions. It's difficult to get in the flow of it at first, because the language is so different, but you'll catch on and fly through it in no time."

"Do you want me to do a graphic organizer or anything?" he asked.

Impressed beyond measure that he thought to ask, I beamed. "Nope."

His face registered amazement. I never asked my class to read anything without doing something on paper to help them process what they were reading and to help me assess what they understood. "No?"

"We'll be talking about the qualities of a hero, so you might want to think about that. Feel free to make a few notes as you go if you want, though."

"Okay." He was stunned.

"*Beowulf,* then." Josh patted Abel on the back. "Got it?"

"Got it," Abel said and returned to his chair.

Josh watched him go. Trying to read his thoughts in his face, I determined that Josh was either very proud of his brother or very proud of himself for raising him.

"He's a good kid," I said.

"Yeah, he is. A little screwed up sometimes . . ."

"I don't know many his age who aren't," I offered as an unsolicited professional opinion.

"Yeah," Josh said, his thoughts obviously having taken flight.

I watched him watching his brother. Abel didn't realize Josh was studying him and Josh wasn't aware that I was contemplating him. My memory banks suddenly spilled over and a line from an old, favorite poem by

Robert Frost forced my eyes from the scene: *An eye is an evil eye which looks in onto a world apart . . ."* My mouth formed the words silently, as a prayer, and I stepped back, separating myself from too-close scrutiny of whatever private meditation there was of Northshore upon Northshore.

Sitting in the slippery plastic chair, I pulled a compact from my purse and quickly inspected my eyes for telltale signs of age and sleeplessness. As satisfied as I could be, I sat back and breathed in the coolish, climate-controlled air and looked around. Airports look as sterile as doctors' offices. I noticed that there wasn't a sign of the holiday season anywhere around.

Might as well hang a banner announcing, THESE CHEERLESS WALLS BROUGHT TO YOU THIS SEASON BY THE ACLU, I thought, shaking my head at the now seemingly annual brouhaha over whether one should say "Merry Christmas" or not.

It was December 23. Sitting on the floor with Nanna the night before with the Christmas tree blinking brightly and the fireplace blazing, opening gifts and listening to her recite "The Night Before Christmas," I was afraid nostalgia and sentimentality would override my excitement about the trip. However, I found myself strangely at peace.

We boarded the plane on time and took off as scheduled. I found a window seat near the rear of the plane. I had tried to ascertain whether or not everyone involved with the team was on the flight, but having no real background knowledge about the sport I couldn't guess. There seemed to be more people than I had seen players on the ice on that snow day, so I assumed that coaches and others were along. Not that it mattered. Until I heard Josh's voice up front.

"Guys, I want to introduce you to someone." A relative hush fell over the burly crowd. "Patricia Smythe"—he was searching for me on tiptoe—"she's Abe's English tutor for the trip."

Someone was pointing me out and I waved a very small wave. I spotted Abel a couple of rows up, sliding lower in his seat as someone in the front sang out, "Abel's got a nanny!" and others let out catcalls. Not since I turned thirty had I given place to the notion that a random whistle or call was directed at me. I never considered myself a very sexy person. However, in this context and with Abel so nearby, I felt embarrassed and visions of purple and green argyle flashed in my head.

Those seated in front and beside me greeted me and apologized for their less couth teammates as Josh made his way back to my seat. I had already unpacked my laptop when he sat down next to me.

"Comfortable?"

"Yes, thank you," I said, shifting my leg ever so slightly away from him. He was like a radiator, heat emanating from him.

"I'll introduce you more personally later." He sounded apologetic. "I just thought some of the guys might be wondering. Might think you were a reporter who stowed away or something, what with the laptop and all." He grinned.

"Oh, I just thought I'd get a little work done," I explained, closing the top and trying to appear as if his presence was more important than anything else at that moment.

"Well, I won't keep you," he said as he stood.

"Oh, it's okay," I said too quickly.

He smiled like he had just gotten the punch line of a joke. "You go ahead, I brought some reading to catch up on myself. I'm right there"—he pointed—"if you need anything."

"Thanks," I said weakly.

"Have a good flight."

He stepped one row forward and sat on the aisle seat where I could see him in profile. He was a matter of a few feet away. I could still smell him. I watched him fish in his bag for something, watched him stretch his legs out in front of him before putting on a pair of very stylish, thin, gold wire-rimmed glasses and opening a beat-up paperback. I couldn't see the title.

Shaking my head to clear my mind of the enticements that had filled it up, I returned to my work. It wasn't the work Josh thought I was doing, though, it was personal work. My journal.

It's very in vogue to journal now, I'm told. I never would have thought I had much to say until I took an evening course at the community college back in the spring.

It was called Recording a Life in Journals and Memoir. For seven Wednesdays from 7–9 P.M., I joined twelve other men and women, ranging in age from twenty-six to seventy-three, and ranging in occupation from administrative assistant to retired accountant, as Sunny Daws, MFA, taught us the difference between crafting history and journaling, the luxuries of creative nonfiction, and the ethical questions surrounding revisionism. We wrote. We read each other's writings. We critiqued and commented and compared.

Sunny suggested we limit the focus of our writings to a single theme, time, or meaningful event in our lives to begin with. The obvious for me would have been my mother's death, but unwilling to revisit the heartache I opted for another theme: Life as an adult literacy coach.

It's what I do at night. It's my superhero persona. Even Nanna doesn't know. When I'm out every Thursday evening, she assumes I'm grocery shopping or involved in some other menial but necessary task; but in reality I'm sitting in a circle in the Fellowship Hall at LaFayette Community Church listening to men and women in their thirties and forties—and fifties sometimes—read aloud and supplying them with strategies for improving their skills. It's the most gratifying thing I've ever done. They call me Pat in the Hat because I promised to wear a red-and-white-striped chapeau straight out of Seuss' book for the rest of the class whenever someone in the group has a reading revelation—or a breakthrough moment. They like it. So do I.

Accepting this trip had necessitated my turning over my small but determined group to another coach, Hillary, while I was gone. We had our Christmas party early so that I wouldn't have to miss it. They insisted. There was cake and punch and nuts and mints. Family members joined them and I got to meet wives, husbands, children, and grandchildren. It was the best party of the season. There were gifts too. Each one received a new book from me. I took a cue from my childhood piano teacher who, each year at Christmas, selected a new piece of sheet music for me to learn—one that was just a little beyond my ability, but not out of reach. They gave me a pair of red-and-white-striped mittens and a matching scarf. These I packed with care and promised to wear on my trip. I made no promises about the hat. They had each signed a card with wishes for the season and the new year. I told them I would miss them and I knew that I would.

Lost in thought, I hadn't realized that I was staring straight at Josh. When he glanced over his shoulder and our eyes met I thought I'd die. Suddenly, I was aware of the sounds all around me. At least two octaves were represented in the half-dozen snores reverberating through the plane. I could see two card games going on from my vantage point, the flittering sound of a shuffle and the shulsh-shulsh of the deal were surprisingly clear. Or, were my senses just heightened?

Could be the altitude. But it could be something else. Josh winked and smiled before returning to his book. I edged farther away from his line of vision, a red alert sounding in my brain: *Don't be stupid, Patricia. Don't be stupid.*

But what exactly was I so afraid of that would make me appear stupid? I chastised myself for the adolescent assumption that no good-looking person of the opposite sex would ever actually find me attractive. I braved a peek around the seat again, and our eyes met. Was this some juvenile game of "caught you looking?" I sucked in a deep breath, set my laptop aside and stood. I wasn't going to let Josh turn me into a fawning little girl. Yes, he was very attractive and, seemingly, very nice. Yes, I could let myself get lost fairly easy in a hockey fantasy of sorts, but I am a grown woman. I'm bright, confident—*am I?*—capable and attractive—*yes, I am.* There's nothing inferior about me; I shouldn't have to feel as if I'm hiding from the world or I think myself unworthy of the attention of a fine man like Josh Northshore.

My legs were moving before my brain caught up and when it arrived a few seconds later, I was standing in front of him. He lowered his book and looked up into my face. I hate to say it but time really did stand still. At least, my brain froze momentarily and, along with it, the ability to speak.

"Everything okay?" he asked, an amused and devilish look in his eyes.

"Just needed to stretch," I heard my voice come from outer space somewhere. "What are you reading?" I asked, my sense of time and place crashing in on me and my legs becoming a bit wobbly.

"*The Broker.*" He held it up for me to see.

"Grisham," I said. "I love his books. I read that one last summer. It's my favorite of the thrillers."

Josh scooted to the inside seat and patted the spot next to him. I took the seat happily.

"This is my first," he said.

"You chose well. So, you like espionage?"

"Can you say that word on a plane?" He looked around quickly before breaking into a laugh. "Yeah, I do. Thrill of the chase, I guess." That teasing glint returned to his sparkling eyes.

I let it lay, not wishing to become engaged in a back and forth game of subtleties and find myself second-guessing everything he said or overanalyzing everything I said for the next couple of weeks. "Well, I don't want to interrupt. I'll let you get back to it," I said, standing.

"No, stay a minute." I sat back down. "What were you working on so hard back there?"

"Oh, just some stuff for a class I teach." I shrugged it off, unwilling to disclose my secret identity to him just yet.

"One of your English classes?"

"Uh-huh," I said as nonchalantly as possible and simultaneously justifying to myself my shading of the truth. "When do we land?" I asked, turning the subject.

"About half an hour," he said, consulting his watch.

"Then what?"

"Check in, relax a bit. Practice a bit. Game tonight."

"I'm looking forward to it."

"To the game?" he asked, somewhat surprised. "Are you a fan so soon?"

"Just curious. My grandmother got me a great gift for Christmas. I'm just anxious to try it out."

"What? Pair of skates? A stick?"

I laughed. *"A Girl's Guide to Hockey.* It's got the prettiest pink cover and tabbed sections for quick reference."

My remarks had the desired effect. His chin lifted and his eyes closed, his laugh bubbled up like a spring and his curls tickled the rolled collar of his sweater. I could feel my smile in my ears. I made him laugh.

"I'll have to take a look at it, see if it's accurate. Wouldn't want you mistaking a face-off for a face-lift or something like that."

"I'll bring it by sometime," I said, standing again. "Think I'll catch a little nap before we land."

"Sleep tight."

"Thanks."

I reached my seat feeling as if I'd been on a three-day hike through the mountains. My ears were ringing, my forehead was damp, my mouth was dry and I was shaking all over. I leaned my head back against the seat and closed my eyes, trying to block all things Josh from my brain, invoking relaxation and rest. I recited all of Mark Anthony's speech in my mind before my breathing had slowed and my heart rate seemed to return to normal. Then, I fell asleep. I didn't wake until it was time to land.

"Nanna?" I shouted into the phone. There was a commotion behind her small voice and I instinctively tried to be heard over it. "What's all that noise?"

"The band!" I heard her shouting back.

"What band?"

"The band at Mr. O'Malley's party!"

"I thought Mr. O'Malley's party was on Christmas Eve?"

"It was, but he was able to get tickets for the Leon Redbone concert Christmas Eve, so he bumped it up."

"Oh," I said, still perplexed. How do you just bump up a party? "Are many people there?"

"Oh, thousands! It's a rave!"

A rave. A rave? Did my grandmother just say, "a rave?" "I just wanted to tell you that we're in Toronto. The flight was fine."

"Of course it was," she said, not even bothering to feign concern for my benefit. "Why wouldn't it be?"

"Just wanted you to know," I said, somewhat sheepishly now.

"I've got to go, love. Charlene and Mr. Stevenson are starting a conga line!"

Somewhere an orthopedist's Christmas wish is coming true.

"Take care, Patty," she said quickly and hung up,

already off to dance the night away with Charlene and Mr. Stevenson and all the rest of the over seventies.

Patty? Since when did she call me Patty? No one had called me Patty since grade school! And I didn't like it then. I was still staring at the phone in disbelief when someone knocked on my door.

"How's your room?" Josh asked, stepping in.

"Very nice. It's got a great view."

I watched him walk to the window to see for himself. "You're right. Mine overlooks the air conditioning units," he said without a hint of rancor. My mind searched for words to describe him, words that would let me categorize him: Unassuming, down to earth, unpretentious, genuine. He let the curtains fall back together. "I just wanted to check on you."

"I haven't unpacked yet," I explained, shoving the suitcase aside so that he could sit.

"Abe's doing our grunt work," he said, boldly seating himself at the foot of my bed. "Listen, Patricia," he began and I felt an overwhelming sense of anxiety. He was my employer, after all, and our relationship on this trip was business. My mind raced. Had I overstepped a boundary already? Done something to displease him? So trained was I to be ready for snap inspection that my guilt monitor was always at the hair-trigger setting. "I just want to thank you again for this. I know that Abe has a lot of work to catch up on but I hope that you'll be able to enjoy yourself too. It is a holiday after all."

"Thank you," I said softly. He scooted over a few inches and I joined him. "I appreciate that."

"There will be dinners and events. I'd be honored if you would be my guest at those." He looked me straight in the eye.

"Of course," I said, feeling warmth rising to my face as my imagination took flight picturing us on a series of romantic dates.

"Great." That being established, he jumped up and was nearly out the door before I could compose myself. "Oh, and tomorrow night, Abe and I will have Christmas Eve together. We'd like you to be a part of that as well. After all, we stole you from your own family for Christmas."

"Oh, I don't want to intrude," I said in sudden awareness of the tenuous line between professional and personal life. "Abel's your family. Besides, he might not want his English teacher along for Christmas Eve."

"It was his idea," Josh said, stepping back into the hallway. "Tomorrow night, Christmas Eve. Don't make other plans. Okay?"

What other plans could I possibly make in Toronto on Christmas Eve, I wondered? "If you insist," I said weakly, still unsure of the wisdom of the plan.

"I insist," he said, pulling the door closed.

"Well, if you insist," I said into the mirror after he'd gone.

Curious, I thought, that Abel would think to include

me. Was it true? Or, was it just Josh's attempt to make
the invitation more palatable to me?

Before very long, there was the sound of a parade in
the hallway. I went to the door to see what was going
on. Opening it, I saw the team filing past.

"On our way to practice, Teach," the Shakespeare-
quoting center called to me, waving as he passed.

"Good luck. Or, is it, break a leg?"

"Not in hockey," another player said gruffly.

I smiled sheepishly. Josh was bringing up the rear
with Abel in tow. "Hello, Northshore men."

"Hello," Abel said softly.

"Reporting for duty," Josh announced, pressing his
brother toward me. "He's read the assignment you gave
him and is ready to do whatever is next."

"I noticed a coffee shop in the lobby, Abel. Would
you like to bring your books down there? We could discuss heroism over cappuccino," I suggested. "My treat."

"I'll get my book," he said and turned down the hall.

"I'll meet you down there in five," I called after him.

"Thanks," Josh said.

"Just doing my job."

He shook his head slightly, the soft curls moving
gently like leaves blowing in a breeze, and smiled. There
was a warmth behind his eyes, like the heart-tugging
warmth of a little cottage tucked back in the trees on a
cold night, its windows illuminated and welcoming, calling out to anyone who would come. I felt myself totter-

ing dangerously near the edge of romantic indulgence. Frost's verses intermingled with Kincaid's imagery creating an enchanting vision, one I hadn't entertained for a very long time and which startled me enough so that I forced it straight out of my head. "Have a good practice," I said, and turned back to my room, closing the door quickly and watching through the peep hole until he had gone. I fumbled for my anthology and some cash, dizzy and nearly delirious.

Go back to what you know, I chided myself, grabbing my room key and heading for the coffee shop. *Literary analysis, symbolism, parallelism, teaching.* I recited the list like it was a creed. *Enough of this junior high crush stuff. None of that is real. It's an old, better-off-dead dream that never really had a chance. You're here on business, so act like it.*

The elevator carried me down to the vast lobby where men of age wore green jackets and round hats and strolled along with brass carts filled with luggage, where the counters were tall and everything was oversized, where the plants reaching for the skylights were taller than the trees in my back yard. I reoriented myself by the front doors and found the shop I had spotted on the way in, and settled into an overstuffed leather armchair with a cup of creamy coffee, the size of which was perfectly proportioned to the lobby: Really big.

Abel joined me directly and we got down to business. It was an exhilarating discussion. I knew he was bright, just not disciplined. After an hour of defining the qualities of heroes and anti-heroes and of antagonists, I asked him to read a poem for me: Alfred Lord Tennyson's "The Lady of Shallot." I leaned in to hear his voice and soon was lost in the heartbeat of the verse. Abel was a smooth reader. The poet's story of the lovely, lonely woman trapped in a life apart, unknown, unloved, so desperate to have her name cross the lips of some other human being that she is willing to die for it, was one Abel might have connected to his own mother's life. When he reached the last line, we were quiet together. Selfishly, my mind turned to my lost mother and her misguided quest for love. Chasing the somber mood away with the last remaining and now cold dregs of cappuccino, my eyes returned to Abel. He was far away, visiting his own mother, I imagined. Pain too intense for a person of his years left its mark around his eyes and mouth.

Of course. Of course he's thinking of his mother.

Chapter Five

Josh's body slammed against the glass and his beautiful face was smashed there in front of me. I jumped back, startled, horrified, yet strangely enthralled. Abel laughed at me.

"Where's the call on that?" I asked him, incredulous that the play went on.

"On what?"

"On what?"

"On that? That was nothing."

"Nothing?"

He didn't respond.

"Sure looked like something to me," I muttered. "I'm not sure I like this game."

I looked back at Abel, who was smirking. I consulted my cheat sheet, a three-page document I had worked up with a little online research: A listing of players, a picture taken from the official team site, numbers and positions. The last category still meant very little to me but I figured if I was going to be in such close quarters with these guys it might be nice if I could remember some of their names. And, since I couldn't impose a seating chart on them, this was the best means available.

"What's that?" Abel asked, peeking over my shoulder.

"Notes."

"You're studying at a hockey game?" He rolled his eyes.

I laughed in spite of myself. Abel had just confirmed my long-held belief that students believe their teachers to be exactly who they are in the classroom at all times. They think we always talk in academic terms, grade everything we read, and probably talk to our pets the same way we talk to them.

"Yeah, studying." I elbowed him and handed him my papers.

"What's this?" he said as he flicked through.

"Just trying to learn who everyone is." I smiled.

"Got a pen?"

"You're not going to draw horns and mustaches on them are you?"

"Just the really mean ones," he said and held out his hand.

I fished in my purse and, much to my chagrin, all I could come up with was a red pencil. Abel took it, the smirk on his face growing stronger. He hunched over, a habit I had noted in class, and wrote intently.

A buzzer sounded signaling the end of the first period. I looked at the scoreboard for the first time that evening. I knew I had seen a couple of our guys score, but hadn't noticed whether or not the Maple Leafs had kept up.

"Two-three," I read aloud.

"Here"—Abel handed back my cheat sheet—"study that. I'm going for a hot dog. Want anything?"

"Popcorn would be great." I fished a five from my pocket.

There were no horns, nor mustaches drawn on in red. Instead, Abel had written brief biographies and personal nicknames by various players. I read:

Sam Raymond aka "Samson": #19, Goalie—has a son about my age named Ted, met him once; divorced and really mad about it. Ex-wife is Theresa—left him for a baseball player (STOOPID!)

Lyle Sikes aka "Skywalker": #3, Left Wing—about Josh's age. Really cool. Star Wars fan, great artist. Going to design a tattoo for me for my birthday.

James Allen aka. "The Fist": #7, D-man; 3-time Cup winner, tells dirty jokes, may be retiring soon, but no one's supposed to know—don't ask!

Josiah Northshore aka Josh aka "Mt.

Northshore": #22, Right Wing; best guy I know, single, loves dogs—has a Husky named Grendel ☺ thought you should know, went to Northwestern and majored in Romantic Literature (refuses to help me cheat in your class).

Fred Kaster aka "Freddie Kruger": #19, D-man; rookie, likes to play practical jokes—watch out. Single, kind of a jerk to women—watch for his name in the tabloids.

David Brickman aka "The Brick Man": #33, Goalie; don't know much about him—he never talks to me. Josh says he's an ok guy, though.

I grinned reading his notes. He seemed to be offering me a cross between team profiles and dating service information. I read his comments on his brother a second time. How many eighteen-year-old boys would say their older brother is the best guy they know? I wondered. I was certain of the truth of it, though. There's more to Josh than meets the eye. I had reached that conclusion the night he drove me to the Loop in a powder-blue Mustang.

"What's that machine?" I asked Abel as he handed me my popcorn.

"Zamboni," he said around a bite of hot dog.

"Zamboni?"

"Yeah."

"What's a Zamboni?"

"It cleans the ice."

"Cleans it?" I took another look. "I wish they made models for kitchen floors."

"Yeah, I'd like to see Mrs. Flannery driving one of those around the kitchen." He laughed. "You're funny," he said, around a huge bite of hot dog.

Funny? Was it a compliment or a smarmy teenager remark? I decided to take it at face value. Abel had a great laugh, just like his brother's. It was a pity he didn't find reason to laugh more often. What I knew of him from school was very unlike this road-trip Abel. He was sullen, quiet, not willing to be vulnerable. Now, in this atmosphere, one-on-one, he was pleasant to be around. I found I liked him. I was glad I came along.

I pulled off my red-and-white-striped mittens to eat my buttery popcorn.

"Cool mittens." He smirked.

"You think?"

"Not so much." He raised an eyebrow. "They look kind of like a little girl's."

"Well, they were a gift."

"From your boyfriend?"

"Boyfriend?" I almost choked.

"Yeah."

"No, not from a boyfriend. Just from some friends. They were a joke, kind of."

"Oh. Good joke."

The Zamboni made its last pass over the ice, leaving it a perfect and shining sheet of glass. The buzzer sounded and the teams reappeared looking refreshed.

"Second period's always the best," Abel offered.

"Why?" *They all seem alike to me.*

"Just is," he said, leaning forward and wiping his hands on his jeans.

"Oh," I said with disappointment.

I consulted my list quickly and tried to spot the players Abel had introduced me to. Josh was easy to find now that I was used to looking for his number. Before they met at the middle of the rink, I had located three of the others: The Brick Man who stood "between the pipes"—a term I had heard used in context of the goalie and was now trying to incorporate into my developing hockey vocabulary—number three Lyle "Skywalker" and number seven James "The Fist." The ref sounded his whistle and a player from each team hunched down waiting for the puck to drop. The eyes of the crowd were riveted.

The game was on in a matter of seconds. The Maple Leafs started on the power play since at the end of the first period one of the Showboats had been penalized for high sticking. Toronto scored before time ran out and the Showboats were back to full strength—another term I had learned by listening to the game announcers and which, every time I heard it, made me think strong coffee—but down by two.

Josh was on and off the ice several times in a matter of minutes. I was amazed at how quickly the coach changed players. It seemed to me that no one had a chance to really hit his stride. Time-out was called by St. Louis and when play began again, Josh was on the ice.

The crowd was still very appealing to me. There seemed to be a never-ending supply of interesting things to hear and see—along with some blatantly embarrassing things to hear and see—but it seemed that every time I indulged myself in eavesdropping or having a look around, I missed something either amazing or devastating on the ice. In fact, the Showboats scored three times before the second period ended and I missed all three! I vowed that in the third period, I would keep my eye on the puck. Hockey was obviously not a game for the casual observer. It calls for complete attention from the stands.

"Well, coach won't be happy," Abel speculated.

"Why? We're winning." I consulted the scoreboard even as I spoke, afraid I had looked at it wrongly. No, five-four, visitors.

"Too close," Abel said.

"Really?"

"Yeah, really. There's no room for error."

"It does all happen pretty fast."

"Just like life," Abel said and excused himself for another trip to concessions.

"No room for error, just like life," I considered. *Out of the mouths of babes.*

"Showboats suck!" A rough voice sounded close by my ear and the sickening smell of beer and cigarettes wafted across my face.

My ear felt warm and wet. I turned and found myself face to face with a large man in a Maple Leafs jersey, holding a cup of beer which sloshed dangerously close to my arm. I smiled weakly.

"Showboats suck!" he repeated, his face reddening with the exertion.

I turned back around and scanned the concourse for Abel.

"Showboats suck! Showboats suck! Showboats suck!" I could see him from the corner of my eye waving his beer over his head and inciting the crowd to riot.

They happily took up the chant. I sunk lower in my seat. Abel came back, dodging a balled-up napkin as it flew past him. He sat down, gooey nachos in hand and started eating.

I was amazed. He was completely oblivious to what was going on around us. Shouldn't we be looking for a way out or something? You hear about people getting trampled in riots at soccer games all the time. This was close enough to trampling for me. Abel, completely unconcerned, crunched his chips as I watched him.

"Bite?" he asked, offering the tray.

"No, thanks."

"Hey, look!"—he lit up, pointing—"We're on the Jumbotron. Wave!"

I followed his gaze to the giant screen on the scoreboard. There we were, two little specks in a sea of red-faced fans yelling, "Showboats suck!" Abel waved. I didn't. He picked up my hand and waved it for me, laughing.

Thankfully, the buzzer calling the players to center ice pierced the mounting chant and life in the stands returned to normal. The third period was intense. I know Abel said the second was the best, but watching the guys play now was like watching a student with a B+ trying desperately for the A-. Dedication to the task, that's what I was witnessing. There was a decided finesse in their play, a determination on each face to stay aware of every player and his position on the ice and to be ready. The tension was fantastic, thrilling. I found myself leaning forward in anticipation of the next play, though I didn't understand the game yet.

Earlier in the evening, I had soaked in a hot bath, trying to wash away the disturbing memories that had gathered around me during my tutoring session with Abel, and had reached for the *Girl's Guide*. I perused its sections, lingering long enough to read some through. I realized nothing of import burrowed itself into my awareness, though, as I watched the last period unfold. I knew enough to cheer when we scored, and enough to recognize checking when I saw it. That was about it.

The game ended seven-six to the Showboats. The arena emptied surprisingly quickly and Abel and I caught a taxi to the hotel.

"What did you think?" he asked.

"It was fun," I said, considering other adjectives, but opting for the simplest expression. I wasn't really sure what I thought, but fun seemed safe. "Why don't you play?"

"I don't know."

"Don't you think you'd like it?"

"Why should I?" He began to sound a little defensive.

"I don't know. I guess because you enjoy the game. Why else do people play sports?"

"I don't really care about it, you know. Not like Josh does. It's just a stupid game," he said and turned his face toward the window, effectively closing the subject.

I wondered what nerve I had touched with him. Maybe a bit of sibling rivalry? Resentment that the game took so much of his brother away from him? Especially in those college years when he was left alone to deal with his mother?

Better not to make too many assumptions, I thought and turned to the safer subject of schoolwork. "Did you get started on your paper this afternoon?" I asked.

"Just a few notes," he said, still staring out the window.

We pulled into the circle drive at our hotel. "If you need any help, let me know," I said, but Abel was out of the car and heading toward the doors before I could pay the driver. I considered running to catch up but hung back instead, lingering in the lobby and thumbing through a visitor's guide until the elevator doors closed and he was on his way up.

I couldn't imagine what I had said to provoke him so, but whatever it was, I certainly planned to steer clear of the idea of Abel playing hockey. Heading for the elevator after allowing enough time for Abel to get to his room, I noticed the television behind the concierge. The local sportscaster was reporting on the game I'd just seen.

"Hockey fan?" the man behind the desk asked me.

"No," I said without thinking. The puzzled look on his face was priceless as he looked from the screen to me in my Showboats sweatshirt. "Oh, well, kind of. I just came from the game."

"Are you with the team?" he asked, gesturing toward the floors above. "The Showboats?"

"I'm a schoolteacher. I'm tutoring one of their brothers."

He returned to the news without comment or question. I slipped away to the elevator. I turned to look at my face in the mirrored wall. My skin always seems to look blotchy after I've been in a crowd. I was wiping at a mysterious smudge on my cheek when the doors opened again.

"Patricia," Josh said, stepping onto the elevator. "Where's Abe?"

"Gone on up to his room."

Several other members of the team entered and I felt the floor of the elevator bounce as each stepped on. My palms were sweating. I am slightly claustrophobic and have a real fear of elevators. Josh's arm was against mine.

"Did you like the game?" he asked, smiling proudly.

"I did. It was interesting." I meant it as a compliment.

"Interesting?" Seth, the center and Shakespeare expert leaned forward and winked at me. "Is that an English teacher's way of saying, 'Kickin'?'"

"Yeah." I smiled at him. "It was kickin'."

Seth laughed warmly and I felt a blush rising to my cheeks. Was it my imagination, or was Josh standing closer than was necessary?

"You coming to dinner, Teach?" another asked.

Which one is he? Which one is he? The one who plays practical jokes! Kaster? Fred Kaster. "Thanks, Fred," I said, smothering the name a little bit just in case. "I think I'll turn in early."

"Aw, come on," a gruff voice sounded on the other side of the elevator. "It's not a school night or something." It was James Allen, the dirty-joke-telling, soon-to-be retiree.

"No, but thanks," I said decidedly.

"My treat," Josh whispered by my ear.

"I really should get a little work done," I whispered back.

"Be a sport," he said, nudging me gently. "Abel can come along as your chaperone." He winked.

"I'm not afraid of you." I felt an idiot grin spreading across my face.

"Oh, be afraid," another voice cut in. "Be very afraid."

There was raucous laughter as the doors opened and the elevator emptied. I stood facing Josh.

"Be my guest? You have to eat," he prodded.

"Okay. Just give me a few minutes to change."

"Nothing too fancy. It's just a bar and grill."

He waited until I was safe inside my room. "Pick you up in half an hour," he called after me.

I leaned against the door of the room, my head dizzy and my face flushed. Dinner with a professional hockey team. What was I thinking? I was way out of my depth. Academia had been my sanctuary, my retreat. Single white female seeks courtly love with lofty intellectual. *Is that really who I am? Is that who I set out to be? Is it what I wanted? Do I want it now?* A sickening sweat was beading up on my brow and I hurried to the small hotel closet to find something suitable for dinner in a hotel bar and grill. A pair of wine-colored cords and a . . . and what? I moved hangers to the side one at a time, inspecting the end result of my haphazard packing. Gray? Too plain. Black? Too stark. My complexion was always fair, but seemed downright chalky to me lately. Too many hours with my nose stuck in a book or with my head bent over paperwork. Pink? Maybe. Cream? Definitely.

I pulled the soft, fuzzy twin set from the closet and tossed it to the bed alongside the pants. Pulling off my blue tribute-to-the-team sweater, I caught sight of myself in the mirror. Not bad, I considered, turning to the front and smoothing my hands down my stomach. Not bad at all. I reached for the twin set and was just starting to pull it over my head when the row of exotically scented lotions caught my eye: Chai, Tiger Lily, and Asian Mystery.

"Nanna has a penchant for the Orient," I observed, opening the lid of the first bottle and sniffing cautiously. "Chai," I said, reading the label. "A sweet blend of vanilla and ginger with spice overtones." I sniffed again. "Well, at least I know vanilla." I poured some of the cool cream into my hand, smoothing it over my arms and chest and stomach. There was a knock at the door.

"Just a minute," I called, panicked. He was early. I quickly pulled on the outfit of choice and went to the door.

"I'm early," Josh said, smiling like a kid. "Sorry."

"It's okay," I said, stepping aside to let him in, trying desperately to tame my voice. "I'm almost ready. Just need to pull on shoes and fix my hair."

I went into the bathroom to assess my tresses.

"You have beautiful hair," Josh called to me.

"Thanks," I said, wrestling the curls into submission. "It's just like my mother's. Funny how I always thought it looked good on her and hated it on myself." I reached for my shoes by the door and noted he had seated himself on my bed.

"Well, I like it," he said.

"Thanks."

Josh moved to the side and patted the mattress. I carried my shoes across the expanse of carpeting between us and turned, feeling that now all-too-familiar dizziness that seemed to accompany his presence as I sat down.

"You said casual, right?" I asked nonsensically as I addressed my feet. "Is this okay?"

"You look great."

I smiled at him, sitting up now. I noticed he was wearing a jacket and jeans. "You look great too."

"Thanks. Shall we?"

"Is Abel coming?" I asked as he pulled the door and checked the lock.

"Said he already ordered a pizza." Josh shrugged. "He doesn't like hanging out with the team much."

We started toward the elevator, Josh a half-step behind me. I twisted a stray curl nervously around my finger.

"Oh," he said suddenly, his voice husky and hungry. "What are you wearing?"

I turned to face him. "What do you mean?"

"Your perfume. It's—"

"Is it too strong?" I felt panic rising.

"No," he gushed. "It's wonderful. So unusual. It's . . . very sensual. Heady."

I couldn't stop the smile from spreading across my face any more than I could stop the warmth from racing to the top of my head. I'm sure my ears turned pink.

"It's just a scented lotion," I shrugged casually and turned back toward the elevator. In a moment he was standing behind me, close enough that I could hear his breath, taking in the scent of me like a man parched and happening upon an oasis. I kept my eyes forward until we reached the restaurant, unwilling to let myself in for the brutal mental anguish that would surely follow if I tried to read his face.

"Hey, Teach," Seth called, and waved at us from a corner booth.

I waved back and moved quickly through the crowd, anxious for the relief of a group. I slid in with Josh right behind me, our thighs touching under the table. I was afraid to move; either he would think I was disinterested or he would think I was embarrassed. Though the latter was true, I was determined to be a grownup; I held my ground.

"What's good tonight, James?" Josh leaned nearer, looking at the plate of appetizers set squarely in front of The Fist.

James lifted the plate past me and Josh plucked a stuffed mushroom from the plate, popping it into his mouth whole. I tried to concentrate on the menu, but the heat, either from the register, from my imagination, or from Josh, was befuddling. Quickly I looked for the salad menu. When in doubt, order salad. That's what I always say.

"So, Miss Smythe"—a leering Fred Kaster eyed me from across the table—"you often spend your Christmas breaks tutoring wayward young men?"

I was stunned and certain my face registered my mortification, providing Freddie Kruger just the fuel he needed to get his flame going.

"Can't say I ever had an English teacher I cared to see on the weekend. Then again, can't say I ever had one as"—he searched for the word—"luscious as you."

I laughed right out loud. Luscious? All that mental

effort turned up the word "luscious?" The table quieted. A frown crossed Freddie's face. I tried to stifle my amusement, but just as I was about to succeed, Josh's rich, earthy laugh rang out, bringing me and the rest of the table, except Fred, to ease. Fred turned his eyes toward the stuffed mushrooms and I heard very little out of him for the rest of the night.

My salad, gigantic as it was, looked a trifle compared to the platters of burgers and fries and rings that were brought to our table. The conversation was noisy and incessant. I became privy to a number of team intimacies. For instance, I now know that Lyle Sikes keeps a *Star Wars* ticket stub in his pocket for luck; that Sam Raymond phones his son before each game and they quote the twenty-third Psalm together; and that Josh chews a piece of old bubble gum, which he keeps wrapped in a square of wax paper, seven times on each side of his mouth before going out onto the ice.

"Old bubble gum?" I turned my eyes on him, wrinkling my nose in disgust. "Old bubble gum?"

"Bazooka," he said, taking another bite of his burger.

"Why?"

"The cartoon on the wrapper was about hockey," he answered nonchalantly.

I rolled my eyes.

"Aw, come on, Teach," Seth needled me. "We all have some weird little thing we do. What's yours?"

"I don't play sports," I said, poking my fork at the large bits of lettuce left on my plate.

"No, but you have something. You know you do. Like . . . like what do you do before a first date?"

"That's different."

"No, no it's not," Josh interjected. "It's not different at all. Going out to play a game is important and nerve-wracking, just like a first date."

"So, what do you do?" Seth pressed.

"Pair of special lace panties?" Leering Fred spoke again and I wished I could crush him with some well-crafted sarcasm but I didn't need to. Josh's look alone shut him down for the rest of the evening.

"Come on, give," Sam said.

"Okay." I sighed heavily and lay my fork aside. "Before a first date, I . . ."—I looked around the table at a group of grown men waiting to laugh at me and suddenly I felt a part of the group—"before a first date, I always put a penny in my shoe."

"A penny?" The question echoed around the table.

"Yes, a penny." I grinned. "I once read a story where a man put a penny in his daughter's shoe on her wedding day." They all looked perplexed. "For good luck."

"Do you have a penny in your shoe tonight?" Josh asked, his mouth next to my ear so that the others didn't hear him.

"None of your business," I suggested quietly.

"Well, well." Josh raised his eyebrows.

The general conversation split into several conversations between teammates. Listening to them, I picked up random bits of information. Mostly they talked about hockey. Some talked about family or about Christmas. An hour passed and a few began to excuse themselves back to their rooms or off to a late movie or to a local club. An hour and a half later and Josh and I sat in the big booth alone, surrounded by empty plates and glasses.

"Buy you a coffee?" he asked.

We caught the night manager just as he was getting ready to close up. A generous tip in advance of service afforded us two steaming mugs of freshly brewed coffee and we settled into the chairs by the fireplace in the lobby. As large as it was, the setting was quite intimate. The hustle and bustle of hotel guests checking in had waned and now there was just the background noise of an employee or two tapping away on computer keyboards. The music overhead was clear and the lights dim enough to allow a decent view of the sky through the tall windows.

We sipped our coffee quietly, comfortable in our companionship.

"I had a good time this evening. Thank you," I offered after a few minutes.

"Thank you for joining me." Josh smiled warmly.

"Your teammates are characters."

"Sure are. Did you and Abe have a good day?"

Back to business. "Yes, we did. We read Tennyson. He was very . . . contemplative."

"He gets that way."

He grew quiet again and I was a little less comfortable

than before. There was something about Abel that disturbed Josh. I could tell.

"He seems okay to me," I said after a moment or two.

"What's that?" Josh came back from some far-off world I knew nothing of.

"I said he seems okay to me. Abel, I mean."

"Really?" He leaned toward me, an earnest desire to hear something true and good heavy in his eyes.

"Really."

"Because sometimes he just seems so . . . I don't know. Brooding."

"Teenagers are sulky sometimes. A lot of the time."

"I worry about him."

"You're a good brother," I said, raising the cup to my lips.

"It's Christmas Eve tomorrow."

"So it is." I noted the soft melody of "White Christmas" playing overhead. I hadn't thought about it. The holiday had been lost to me in the midst of packing and traveling.

"I'm sorry you are away from your family for the holiday. I'm glad you're here, though."

"It's okay. My grandmother and I celebrated early. She'll be out painting the town without her fuddy-duddy granddaughter there to hold her back," I said as I set the cup on the coffee table.

"It's good to be with family, though, on the holidays."

"Yes."

"You'll come with us, of course," he said, sitting back in his chair with his pronouncement.

"Come with you where?"

"With Abel and me for Christmas Eve."

"I don't want to intrude."

"Intrude? No, we insist. Tomorrow evening at five. Casual and warm." He stood.

"Are we going to the ice rink?" I asked suspiciously.

"No. But, we will be outside for a while, so bundle up."

I stood and he offered his arm. "May I see you to your room, Miss Smythe?"

"You may," I said, feeling charmed and happy.

Outside my door, Josh took my room key and held the door for me. I stepped inside and turned to face him.

"Did you want to come in for a bit?" I asked hopefully.

"It's late. I won't tonight."

"Sleep well," I almost whispered.

Josh leaned toward me and I felt my stomach lurch with anticipation. My head swooned and I steadied myself against the door frame. When his warm, soft lips brushed my cheek, I stopped breathing.

"Sweet dreams, Patricia," he whispered back, his words rushing my pulse and making me tingle all over.

Chapter Six

"That was Tony Bennett singing 'The Christmas Song.'" The morning disc jockey's voice penetrated my sleepy brain and brought me with a start into the new day. Had last night really happened? A warmth rose to my cheeks before my eyes even came into focus. *Yes, last night really happened. Josh kissed me, if only on the cheek.* I relived the moment: The warmth of his body as he leaned toward me, the feel of the door frame against my back, the gentleness of his lips just grazing my cheek. I felt utterly happy.

Then, my inner cynic made herself known. *It was just a friendly peck on the cheek. It meant nothing. He probably doesn't even remember it now.* I replayed the scene again: Josh had walked me to my room, I offered to let him come in, he declined then he leaned in and kissed me on the cheek. He said, "Sweet dreams, Patricia," and then I watched him go.

It's probably some weird hockey tradition, I thought, stretching and then pulling the covers back up tight. *A superstition of some sort. Kissing your kid brother's tutor on the cheek after a win ensures you won't loose a tooth in the next game.*

Bracing myself for the morning chill of the room, I swung my feet over the edge of the bed and sat up. The light coming through the windows was very bright. How late had I slept?

"It's nine on a snowy Christmas Eve," the radio announcer said brightly, his timing plain eerie.

I drew back the heavy brocade drapes and a wintry vision met my eyes. Everything was covered in a fresh layer of white. I stood a moment until the chill from the glass reached my skin. Shivering, I grabbed my laptop and snuggled back under the covers. Nanna loves e-mail and thanks to free Wi-Fi in the room I was able to send her a Christmas Eve greeting complete with a dancing elf, a link to a Toronto webcam and the question, "Do you see what I see?"

Christmas Eve in Toronto. Christmas Eve in Toronto with Josh Northshore. Christmas Eve in Toronto with a whole hockey team. Christmas Eve in Toronto with a brooding student.

I logged onto my school account and searched my

address book for Abel's address. I find e-mail to be a wonderful means for reminding students of missing assignments.

Abel,

    Merry Christmas Eve morning. Please check out the Web site below for an online edition of Shakespeare's Twelfth Night. *It's not in your anthology, but I thought it would be a good option for us. It's a more pleasant read than* Hamlet. *As you read, keep track of Shakespeare's use of religious allusions. Also, I chose twenty lines to memorize and recite. There are several project activities at the Extras link. Check them out and we'll talk about your choice later.*

    See you this evening.

                             Miss Smythe

"Send," I said, clicking the icon just as the phone rang. "Hello?" I asked hesitantly. Who would be calling me?

"Patricia?" It was a man's voice.

"Yes?"

"It's Josh." He sounded timid, not like himself. His robust, resonant voice sounded softer, unsure.

"Is everything okay?" I asked, sitting bolt upright and laying the laptop aside. I was already reaching for my jeans in case of an emergency.

"Yeah, everything's fine. Why?"

Whew. My heart pounded in my ears and I leaned back against the pillow, closing my eyes and laying my hand across my forehead. "You just sounded upset. I thought something was wrong."

"Sorry," he said, still very serious. "Have you had breakfast?"

"No, not yet."

"I didn't wake you did I?"

"No, I've been awake a while." I omitted that it had been only minutes.

"I forget that the rest of the world doesn't get up as early as I do. I'm so used to it. You're sure I didn't wake you?"

"I'm sure," I said, feeling a giggle rising in my throat. He was so sincere.

"I'd like to buy you breakfast," he said, rushing his words, forcing them, really, so that they ran together.

"You bought me dinner."

"I want to talk to you. I know a great little café just a block away. It's really cold out, so bundle up."

"Okay."

"I'll be at your door in twenty minutes. Is that okay?"

"Sure." I was already scrambling for my toothbrush and a bar of soap.

"Great." He sounded relieved. "See you then."

I'm not a person who takes hours to get ready. My taste in makeup and hair and clothing runs to the natural look, as I prefer to call it. Nanna has tremendous disdain for my fair complexion, which I enhance only with the palest of blushers. She says my ponytail is a rag mop in a ribbon and my clothes look as if I pulled them damp from the hamper and dressed in the dark. I take exception to that one especially. My clothes are neutral, classic and comfortable.

I reached into the closet and took out my fun Christmas sweater. I've had it for years. I love it. It's black with multi-colored striped sleeves and a Grinch-green Christmas tree on the front decorated with big, colorful buttons and topped with an embroidered gold star. I had it halfway over my head when I reconsidered. Maybe the fitted V-neck would be a little more flattering, even if it was a last-minute breakfast date. I was pulling on my boots just as Josh knocked.

"Just a minute," I called, stomping my foot against the floor. My socks were too thick.

I opened the door and there he was. A dream. A trophy. A reward for all the little pleasures I'd never known. "Hi," I said, stepping aside. "Almost ready."

Josh let himself in and closed the door. My bed was unmade.

"You're a restless sleeper," he said.

I couldn't hear him for the blood in my ears as I was bent over pulling strands of unmanageable hair into a band. "What's that?"

"You're a restless sleeper," he repeated, this time gesturing at my rumpled sheets.

"I can't stand how tightly they tuck in the sheets in hotels. I have to be able to get my feet free. I hate feeling pinned down. I'm ready." I slung a purse over my shoulder.

"Coat?" he asked.

He is a gentleman. He took my black wool coat by the shoulders and held it for me. As he snugged it up around my neck, I swear I could feel his breath by my ear. "Do you have gloves?"

"In the pockets." I felt woozy.

I pulled on the red-and-white-striped mittens as we exited the building. Josh chuckled.

"What's funny?" I asked, loving the way his mouth turned up at the corners and his nose wrinkled when he laughs.

"Cool mittens."

"That's what Abel said." I socked him playfully on the arm. He feigned injury then took my arm as we crossed the street.

"You said you wanted to talk," I reminded him. "Is it about Abel? I think he's going to pull it off. I e-mailed him this morning with his next assignment. I deviated from our regular curriculum a bit. I hope you don't mind. It's kind of nice to be able to personalize instruction so much. I just chose a play I thought he'd enjoy."

"No, that's great," Josh said, heartily nodding his approval. "No, I wanted to talk about last night."

I felt a burning rock fall into my stomach. *He takes me to dinner and buys me a coffee, gives me one little kiss on the cheek and now he feels like he has to talk to me about it? How desperate do I look anyway? I'm so embarrassed. What excuse will I give for going back home? Abel and I can continue by e-mail. Correspondence school of sorts. Or virtual classroom as it's called these days. Nanna. I can tell him that Nanna needs me. She's sick. Or her dog got hit by a car. She's getting married on New Year's Eve. Anything! I just have to get out of here.*

"Patricia?" His voice pierced through the parade of insanity marching around my head. "Are you okay?"

"Sure," I said with as much flippancy as I could muster. "Why?"

"You got so quiet." He looked at me strangely. "We're here"—he motioned to the door of the café—"you're sure you're all right?"

"Yes, I'm fine. Just hungry, I think," I lied. There was no way I was going to be able to eat.

The café was crowded. Shiny, red vinyl seats and gray Formica tabletops lined the walls while waitresses who looked as if they had stepped out of Arnold's on "Happy Days" buzzed around with giant circular trays. The smells of coffee and bacon, of eggs and fresh biscuits were heavy. Josh pointed to a booth being vacated by a couple of elderly gentlemen and pressed me toward it.

"Let me get those things for you," a waitress said, reaching past me. "Coffee?"

"Yes, please," I said.

"You?" she asked Josh without looking at him.

"The same."

"Cream's on the table," she said, producing two thick, white ceramic mugs and pouring steaming coffee into them from a foot above without spilling a drop. "Back to take your order in a minute," she said and left without waiting for our reply.

"What's good?" I asked, hiding my face behind the grease-coated laminated menu.

"I like the hash."

"Think I'll go with something a little lighter. The breakfast banana split." I spotted the description of a rather healthy sounding banana and berry yogurt parfait topped with granola.

I looked at him now. His menu was folded and his hands rested placidly on the table. His face was all calm and patience. I felt as if I'd been called into the principal's office to be scolded. What would he say? What would I say? I could play dumb. Turn it around on him, let him think that he's the one who's confused, who got it all wrong. No, I knew I couldn't do that.

"What'll you have?" The waitress reappeared with her order pad.

"I'll have the hash with a side of fried eggs. She'll have the breakfast banana split." He looked across at me to make sure.

"Yes, please."

"Right," said Erin, the waitress whose nametag I had happened to catch. She was gone in an instant without ever having made eye contact.

"You should have ordered something warm on a cold

day," he said, grinning, the warmth of his smile permeating me so that not even an arctic blast could have fazed me.

"I always eat fruit for breakfast. So,"—I lifted the steaming mug to my lips—"what did you want to talk about?" I drowned the question in the hot coffee.

"I wanted to apologize," he said, the sorrow over his sins, whatever they were, casting a veil of grief over his face. "I am so sorry . . ."

I opened my mouth to ask what on earth he thought he had to apologize for. For giving me a Christmas vacation unlike any I had ever had, or probably ever would have again in my life? For giving me a chance to experience teaching in a real and personal way, which is nearly impossible in the classroom? For introducing me to his friends and colleagues? For inviting me along on Christmas Eve? For kissing me?

As quickly as the thought occurred, it was met with affirmation. I am not sure to this day whether or not I actually heard him say, "I'm sorry for kissing you last night," or whether I knew so certainly in my soul that these are the words he would say that my mind created the phrase of its own accord.

"Sorry?" I asked, sufficiently surprised. "You don't owe me any apologies." I thought people were looking at us.

"I do. I invited you along on this trip as a professional. I asked you to give up your own personal celebration to come along and help a kid who, frankly, probably doesn't deserve it. I was having such a nice time with you, drinking coffee, chatting in front of the fire, walking you to your room, the way your hair moved on your shoulders, and that scent . . . ," He was losing himself in the memory and igniting a fire in me at the same time.

"Josh." *What was I going to say? Just his name. Over and over again. Josh. Josh. Josh. It's enough.*

"I'm sorry," he said again, locking eyes with me. "I shouldn't have taken advantage of the situation. I should have controlled my impulses. Please accept my apology. It won't happen again. I promise. You're Abel's teacher. I respect that more than you know. I promise."

My heart sank and tears of frustration were building behind my eyes. "Josh," I whispered.

"Hash and a banana split," Erin announced as she plunked down a sizzling skillet of corned beef and potatoes and an embarrassingly large parfait topped with a cherry and a paper Canadian flag on a toothpick. "Eat hearty," she said and disappeared.

I looked at my breakfast and burst out laughing.

"It's . . ."—Josh was suppressing a laugh—"it's very . . . patriotic."

I laughed until the tears that had been threatening rolled down my cheeks. Grateful for the release and determined to make the most of our first and last breakfast together, I plucked the miniature flag from atop the morning monstrosity and licked the whipped cream from the toothpick. "A keepsake," I said.

"Would you like some hash?"

"Only if you'll eat half of this."

"Deal."

"So," I began, trying to dispel the discomfort which seemed to have settled between us, "after the game last night, when Abel and I rode back to the hotel, I mentioned the idea of him playing hockey and he—"

"Turned into a snarling monster?"

"Is snarling monster syndrome common at your house?"

"Not common, but certainly not unheard of."

"Why does the mention of playing hockey bring it on?"

"I've not figured that out entirely," he admitted even as his eyes seemed to search for the answer in some long forgotten vault of important documents. "When I was in college, before Mom's breakdown, I would take Abel out to shoot around a bit. I thought it would be fun. You know? A bonding time."

"But it wasn't," I surmised.

"Not exactly. He'd seem to have fun for a little while, but before long he'd get very quiet and just skate off to the sides and sit. I thought, in my youth and stupidity, he was just jealous because I was good at something and he didn't really have a knack for it, but looking back on it now, I don't think that's the right answer."

"What do you think is the right answer?"

"I think it has something to do with my father."

"Who was he?" I leaned in.

"Pop was an engineer." Josh's wistful smile told on

him. He had fond memories of a man Abel had never met.

"Not on a train." I grinned.

"No. A civil engineer. Bridges, tunnels, stuff like that. Genius."

"You were fifteen." I supplied a detail I recalled from Abel's essay.

"I was fifteen. Abel wasn't born yet. He was away on business. He was just in the wrong place at the wrong time; caught in the crossfire after a robbery. Anyway . . ."

"So, Abel feels the way he does about playing hockey because . . ."

"I think it's because he knows Pop used to play with me when I was a kid. He coached my junior league team. We spent every Saturday on the ice." His smile reappeared with the happy memories. "Every Saturday, we'd get up early, he'd make a stack of pancakes and out the door we'd go, skates, sticks, pucks . . . off to play hockey."

"Abel didn't get that."

"Abel didn't get anything." Josh's focus returned to his breakfast. "Nothing at all. He was robbed of any sort of normal kid life."

"He had you," I offered hopefully.

"Yeah. But, I'm hardly enough to make up for all he lost before he ever had it."

"The past is a funny thing, isn't it?"

"I'm not sure there's really any such thing as the past."

"Whose dog tags are those you keep around the mirror

in your car?" I decided to pursue another line of conversation.

"Julie's," he said flatly.

"Who is Julie?" I was stunned and fearful all at once.

"Julie was my older sister."

"Abel never mentioned a sister." I tried desperately to disguise the crack in my voice.

"She was our half-sister. He never met her either. She was killed in the Gulf War."

"Your father's daughter?"

"From a previous marriage."

"The two of you were close?"

"We were the best of friends. Julie was great. I always looked up to her."

"Well, I'm sorry I mentioned the idea of playing hockey to Abel." I tried to steer the conversation to a close, sensing a need to bring back the comfortable ignorance of each other's personal lives that Josh and I had enjoyed as recently as last night.

"His sulks never last," Josh assured me. "Are you going to eat that or let it melt?" He indicated my rapidly dissolving breakfast.

"Eat it," I said, suddenly hungry.

"Can I have the cherry on top?"

"I guess." I feigned a heavy sigh as he scooped it up and popped it into his mouth, grinning like a kid from ear to ear.

"Thanks." The look of self-satisfaction made me smile in spite of my sadness.

Chapter Seven

At five o'clock that evening, Josh and Abel picked me up as promised. I had spent the day wandering around a used bookstore and writing. Nanna had responded to my earlier e-mail and had added a video of her own: Mr. O'Malley's rave complete with the conga line and a visit from a scantily clad pair of Santa's elves—male and female so no one felt left out. "Well, stuff my stocking," Nanna could be heard to say as the candy-cane-brandishing king of the elves reached for her hand and the world turned upside down. The next view, Nanna's green high-tops and the elf's curly, jingle-bell-bedecked slippers dancing toe to toe was enough to knock at least three Christmases worth of cheer out of me and I shut it off before it got any raunchier. I could hear Nanna now: "Oh, don't be a prude, Patricia. A little romance is good for everyone. Even at my age." My hands instinctively flew to my ears.

"Merry Christmas," Josh said, and nudged Abel who held out a small bouquet of holly and baby's breath tied with a red ribbon.

"Oh, it's beautiful. You shouldn't have. Thank you." I had gifts for each of them, but left them hidden for later. "Where are we going?"

"It's a surprise," Josh said with a wink.

"You said to dress warmly, right?"

"Warmly," Abel repeated with heavy emphasis on ly. "She's an English teacher, all right."

"Warmly," I said for added emphasis.

"Don't forget your mittens," Josh teased.

"Got them right here." I pulled them dramatically from the pocket of my coat. "And . . ."—I let the anticipation build while I went to the closet—"a scarf to match." I produced it with flair.

Abel groaned loudly and Josh socked him on the arm. I laughed at the sight of them. The Northshore men, standing side by side, looked very much like brothers. They were handsome, charming and boyish, having an eager light in their eyes. What was that light? Even Abel seemed more at ease tonight.

I shook my hair out over my collar—I wore it down on purpose and put on an extra layer of Chai lotion—and we went out.

"Where are we going?" I asked as the elevator arrived.

"It's a surprise," Josh said, winking at Abel.

"It's not a local production of *A Christmas Carol,* is it? I've seen some pretty bad Scrooges in my day."

"Nothing like that."

We rode down in silence; when we reached the lobby and the doors came open, it was like a Christmas dream. Bare trees alight with strings of white pinpoints lined the sidewalk in front of the building and up and down the street went horse-drawn carriages driven by men in top hats with holly sprigs in their buttonholes. An orchestration of "The Christmas Song" played overhead and the doorman greeted us warmly, pushing the door open for us as we stepped into a true winter wonderland. My breath caught in my chest and I stood stock still, taking in the sights. Josh and Abel stood beside me. I saw Josh point high up to a lit tower just as I heard its bell begin to chime seven.

"That's the Metropolitan United Church. Have you ever been to a carillon concert before?" Josh asked, his warm breath tickling my ear as he leaned close. His scent warmed me through and through.

I shook my head, mute, astounded by the beauty.

"They have a guest carillonneur this evening. Someone from Germany. Traditional Christmas carols and hymns. Are you up for it? It's about twenty minutes outside."

"Oh, yes," I said, with a shiver of exhilaration.

"You're sure?" he asked, noticing I shook.

"Absolutely. Let's go."

"Come on, Abel," Josh said as he pressed his kid

brother forward. "Just walk that way," he pointed again toward the tower.

We walked along, a trio of shivering, silly Americans acting like a bunch of kids. Abel and Josh tossed loose handfuls of snow at each other as we went. We passed some strolling carolers and the shops along the way beckoned with their warm lights and the inviting smells of hot buttered rum and cider mingled with the nostalgic aroma of fresh-baked gingerbread. It seemed that every person we passed called out "Merry Christmas" to us.

As we came upon the grounds of the church, a crowd had gathered under the stars and under the long shadow of the carillon. An elderly gentleman in a green velvet blazer passed out programs and reminded the audience that there would be a Christmas Eve service immediately after the concert "just through those doors into the sanctuary." We took a seat along a low retaining wall and Josh spread out a stadium blanket across our knees. We huddled in close, my teeth already beginning to chatter.

The night was crisp and the sky was clear. Precisely at 7:10, a single note rang out across the lawn and all eyes went up. It was dizzying. The medley of seasonal compositions produced in me a sense of belonging even though I was among strangers. The crescendos rose over the snowy scene, a praise to the babe whose birth they heralded. Even children hushed themselves, nestling in against their mothers, and wondering at the kaleidoscopic blending of sights and sounds. As the familiar Hallelujah chorus from Handel's "Messiah" rang joyously, I felt a lump rising in my throat and a tear escaped, leaving a frozen trail down my cheek. I had not celebrated Christmas this way for many years.

"Thank you," I whispered. Josh answered by squeezing my shoulder. I had not noticed until that point that his arm was wrapped protectively around me. "Thank you," I said again, with a silent prayer as the final notes sounded.

There was a momentary hush. Not a sound could be heard. Those who had gathered here sat in utter awe, breathless. Then, from the front of the lawn, a single person could be heard applauding, softly at first, tentatively, as if he was afraid of arousing the anger of some silent worshipper. Another took it up and soon we all stood in appreciation of our unseen host who finally appeared high above us at a small window.

The crowd rolled like a gentle wave across the lawn in the direction of the church. Josh picked up the blanket and looked at me expectantly. "What did you think?"

"It was beautiful," I stammered.

"Good," he said, a smile lighting at the corners of his mouth. "Let's go inside where it's warm."

Inside? He offered his elbow and before I knew what was happening, I was being conducted across the lawn toward the church.

"Are you Methodist?" was all I could think to ask.

"No," Josh said casually, as if it didn't really matter

tonight; and, maybe it didn't matter at all. "Grab us a seat, Abe," he called to Abel who was several steps ahead of us.

"Is this okay?" Josh asked.

"Sure."

"I guess I should have asked you. I just didn't think of it. It's our tradition."

"It's fine. Let's go."

To tell the truth, except for the Fellowship Hall where my literacy group met, I hadn't been inside a church since my mother's funeral and I wasn't crazy about going in now. As we stepped across the threshold, my stomach felt hot and sick.

The sanctuary was dark, lit by many candles held by many worshippers and by many more candles on pine-draped stands around the room. A choir sang "O, Holy Night" softly from the loft and a living nativity scene graced the stage.

The pastor appeared at the podium. "Merry Christmas," he said.

"Merry Christmas," the congregants responded.

"This evening we celebrate Christmas. A familiar story is recorded in the gospel of Luke. Here we read . . ."

I listened as the pastor spoke about humility, humanity and divinity, of love and of glory. Then, he stepped down.

A woman about my age approached a microphone set just behind the manger scene and, while the Holy Family prayed in the blue spotlight, she sang. I didn't know the song, the words of which were strange yet marvelous. The voices of all wonderers met hers in that song as our questions passed her lips. "Why take He on our flesh and for our lives give His own? Why stand I thus apart from Him whom my soul has ever known?"

Whom my soul has ever known. My English teacher's mind turned the phrase over and over. *Whom my soul has ever known . . .*

When the pastor's disembodied voice invited us to the holy Communion, Josh and Abel stood to go forward. I remained in my seat, unsure and uneasy. Row after row of worshippers went to the front to receive the blessing of the sacraments. I watched them one by one as they took the bread and the wine with reverence and with an uncommon joy.

The pastor pronounced the benediction and the choir sang, "The Lord Bless You and Keep You," as the congregants greeted one another with hugs and hearty handshakes, wishing each other Merry Christmases and blessed New Years. I followed Josh and Abel through the crowd and back onto the lawn.

"Wow," I said, once we were outside, "that was really beautiful."

"It was, wasn't it?" Josh answered. Abel was several paces ahead of us. "I hope you weren't too uncomfortable."

"No. Why?"

"I don't know. You just seemed very quiet. Abe and I always attend Christmas Eve services wherever we are.

I hope I wasn't too presumptuous. We just wanted you along with us tonight."

"It was a beautiful service," I said, feeling suddenly and inexplicably sad. "I haven't been to church in a long time."

"Why not?" Josh took my arm as we crossed the street.

"I don't know. I quit going after my mother died."

"Oh," Josh said. He wasn't going to judge me.

"Anyway, thank you." I tried to force a cheerful tone. "I will always remember Christmas in Toronto."

"I'm glad. And, it just gets better," he announced as we arrived back at the hotel.

"What do you mean?"

"Santa delivered something for you today. Asked me to give it to you. Come up?" he asked, a twinkle in his eye.

"Sure. Only, Santa dropped gifts for you and for Abel in my room earlier. I promised him I'd get them to you. I'll be up in a few minutes."

A couple of days earlier, I had gone online in hopes of coming up with a quick couple of gifts for the Northshore brothers. I felt a little strange about giving a Christmas present to a student, but since I was being included as a part of his family for the holiday, it seemed appropriate. I'm always extravagant at Christmas but could be even more so this year what with the extra tutoring money I was earning. I grabbed up the two packages, neatly wrapped in green-and-red striped foil and tied with gold ribbons and fluffed my hair before heading to Josh's suite.

The hotel seemed very quiet. Earlier in the day, I had seen several of the team going in and out. Tonight, however, the hallways were deserted. It seemed everyone had somewhere to be. Or, maybe they were just hiding out behind closed doors watching colorized versions of classic Christmas movies and feeling homesick. This last thought made me incredibly sad; but when Josh opened the door and I stepped into his suite, I forgot everything except how good it felt to be in his company.

Jimmy Stewart's long, thin frame graced the television screen and there was a tabletop Christmas tree standing under the window.

"Abe, turn it off," Josh said as he closed the door. "We have company."

"Oh, I love Jimmy Stewart," I said.

"Is it okay?" Abel asked hopefully, remote already poised in his hand.

"You're sure?" Josh asked me.

"I'm sure."

The screen brought the town of Bedford Falls back to life. I placed the presents under the tree then joined Josh on the loveseat. Abel was stretched out across the floor, propped up on pillows.

"I remember the first time I saw this movie," I said.

"How old were you?" Josh asked.

"Seven."

"Seven years old. What were you like when you were seven?"

"I was a scaredy cat when I was seven."

"No." Josh shook his head. "Not likely. Not someone as confident as you."

"Confident?"

"Sure," he said without further explanation.

"Well, I was a scaredy cat then. I was afraid of everything. Dr. Seuss books gave me nightmares."

"Really?"

"Really. I loved the rhymes. I've always loved to play with words. But the illustrations were so bizarre that I just couldn't stand it. I would beg my mother to read them to me, but I'd keep my eyes closed the whole time."

"What else?" He leaned in so we could speak in confidence.

"I hated school."

"You're a teacher."

"I know. But, I really hated school. I got sick every single morning of first grade."

"Why?"

"I think it was because my mother and I had a very quiet household. I'm an only child and it was just the two of us. At school, there was always noise and activity. I just didn't know how to cope."

"What did your mother do?"

"She cried a lot." I shrugged. "And she told me things like, 'Be brave,' and 'You can do anything you set your mind to.'"

"Standard mom stuff. My mother used to say the same things to me about hockey."

At this, Abel's attention was temporarily diverted from the television. That he was eavesdropping was obvious to me, but Josh went on as if we were all alone.

"She used to tell me that I was going places in this life. 'Josiah,' she'd say, 'I want you to do whatever it takes to be the best. Knock yourself out to be the best. That's all that counts.'"

Abel, suddenly fearful of appearing too interested in the conversation, turned his eyes back to the screen where Donna Reed was racing through the front door with snow blowing in after her.

"Is that why you're where you are today?" I asked, feeling uneasy about Abel. This all had to be very hard for him—this season, this lifestyle.

"I don't know. I mean, it would be easy to say that, because not many people make it without someone encouraging them along the way. But, it wasn't really encouragement."

"What was it?"

"It was more like she was talking to herself, not to me."

"How so?"

"Well, she never really looked me in the eye. She always seemed to be looking past me. You know what I mean? Like whoever she was talking to was standing right over my shoulder. I don't know."

The sounds of "Auld Lang Syne" and a tinkling little

bell announced the end of the movie and Abel clicked off the set.

"Presents?" he asked, stretching and yawning.

"Presents," Josh agreed. "Did you believe in Santa when you were seven?"

"Yes," I said. "I did. Did you?"

"Did I? I still do." He winked.

"Santa shows up every year at our house," Abel offered, folding his legs beneath him in some impossible yoga-like pose and pressing himself up without any apparent effort. "Right, Josh?"

"Sure does. Why, look!" Josh pointed toward the tree. "He's already been here tonight."

I laughed, as the poem says, in spite of myself, as Josh, a hockey player with a perfectly chiseled physique, donned a Santa hat and commenced to passing out packages, all the while whistling "Santa Claus Is Coming To Town."

"To Abel, from Santa," he said, handing Abel a rather large and seemingly heavy box wrapped in blue paper with silver snowflakes. "Direct from the North Pole," Josh added. "Guess you've been good this year."

Abel looked sheepish all of a sudden. He glanced at me and smiled weakly. He didn't open his gift. Josh reached under the tree again and deposited a tiny package wrapped in gold foil and tied with a red velvet bow on the coffee table in front of me.

"For Miss Patricia Smythe. Care of Josh and Abel

Northshore. Merry Christmas." He grinned and Abel set his still unopened present aside.

"Open it," Abel said.

"Now?" I felt embarrassed.

"Go ahead," Josh said, sitting down beside me.

I untied the bow and slid it over the corners of the box, and loosened the tape at the ends. I felt like Charlie opening his bar of chocolate. What could be inside? It was such a tiny box! I let the paper fall to my lap and gently lifted the top off the box. There were no identifying marks on the package, no sticker with a department store name or a brand, nothing to indicate the contents. Inside, there was a layer of white cotton and underneath it, a very delicate brooch.

"It's beautiful," I said, lifting it from its box. The pewter had been recently shined and its intricately cut edges caught the light. It was in the shape of a heart with a most unusual arrow through it. "I've never seen a pin like this," I breathed, holding it up against my sweater. "Thank you."

"It's an ink pen," Abel said.

"What?" I took it down to look at it again.

"Here," Josh reached across my lap and tugged at the arrow revealing a little ink pen.

"Oh, my goodness! It's so delicate! Where did you find it?"

"A little antique shop a few blocks over. Do you like it?"

"I love it. It's the most extraordinary gift I've ever been given. Thank you."

"There's another," Abel said.

"Another?" Josh asked, surprised.

"Hang on." He jumped up and disappeared.

"What's he doing?" I asked, pinning the brooch to my sweater.

"I don't know. The kid has secrets."

Abel returned with another package, this one wrapped in plain white tissue paper and tied with a piece of tinsel. On the top in black ink was written:

To Miss Smythe. Merry Christmas and thanks for the second chance. Abel.

"Abel, you didn't need to do that," I said, accepting this precious present from him.

"I know." He shrugged, trying to extinguish any emotion that might be threatening. "I just saw it."

"When did you do this?" Josh asked, incredulous, as I broke the tinsel and pulled the tissue aside.

"I went to the mall with Skywalker yesterday while you were working out."

"The Writings of Alexander Pope." I read the spine of the nicely bound book and ran my fingers over its cover. "Thank you, Abel."

"I remembered you saying you liked his stuff once."

"I do. Very much. Thank you. What a nice thought."

There was an uncomfortable moment just long enough

for the lights on the tree to blink once and then I was on my feet. "Well, Santa left gifts for the two of you at my room today too."

I retrieved the identically wrapped packages and handed them to the brothers.

"You first," Josh said.

"Okay." Abel reached for the blue snowflake box, which he had set aside earlier.

I returned to my seat and watched Josh watching Abel. The anticipation was bright in his face. I turned to see what it would be.

"Awesome! Dude, thanks!" Abel practically gushed as he pulled a skateboard from the box.

"Is it the right kind?" Josh asked, excitedly.

"Yeah. Dude, Kyle is going to be so jealous. Thanks, Josh."

"Thank Santa," Josh slugged his brother in the arm. "Merry Christmas."

After that, I wasn't sure what Abel would think of my gift but he tore into it with great gusto.

"I hope you don't mind," I said softly to Josh as Abel pulled the tickets from the box. "They are going to be in Seattle at the same time we are . . ."

My explanation was lost in a shout of surprise. "No way! No freakin' way!" Abel was waving the tickets at Josh. "Did you know?"

"What is it?" Josh asked trying to extricate the tickets from his brother's hand. "Who's in Seattle?"

"Aerosmith," I said.

"No way!" Josh shouted, grabbing the tickets and looking at them.

"And on New Year's Eve! That is too cool, Miss Smythe. Thank you."

"There are only two tickets here," Josh said, still staring at the apparently inspired gift in his hands.

"Well, yes," I said. "I thought Abel would like to take someone along."

"If it was three, we could all go," my student said, squeezing onto the loveseat next to his brother and peering over the large shoulder to the tickets.

"You shouldn't have," Josh said. "This is too much."

"Yeah," Abel agreed. "I thought teachers were underpaid."

At this, Josh elbowed Abel in the ribs and scowled.

"Just joking. Thanks again, Miss Smythe. This is kickin'."

"You're welcome," I said, feeling smug.

"Now you." Abel pointed to Josh's unopened gift.

"This better be something much less 'kickin',' " Josh said, eyeing me suspiciously.

I watched his amazingly nimble fingers peel away the gift wrap and my mind threatened to wander too far into fantasy; I believe my cheeks even flushed. *Stop it, Patricia, don't be such an adolescent.*

The box opened, Josh reached in and lifted out from amidst the tissue, the authentic special edition gear shift knob for a 1968 Mustang. "Merry Christmas," I said softly as I watched him holding the treasure, admiring it in the soft lights of the Christmas tree.

"Where on earth did you find this?" he asked, amazed.

"Internet shopping is truly a wondrous experience," I said with a shrug.

"Thank you. This is wonderful."

"I'm glad you like it." I grinned.

"Shall we have some eggnog?" Josh asked, tossing the knob lightly up and catching it before setting it like a trophy on the table.

"Eggnog?" Abel groaned. "I hate eggnog."

"Are you kidding me?" I gasped in mock astonishment. "It's a holiday classic."

"What does Abe know from classic?" Josh ribbed.

Abel held his heart and fell to the floor. "Oh, your insults hurt so much! Listen, I know classic, bro," he said sitting up. "And for your information, classic and old are two entirely different things." He ended his good-humored tirade by smacking his gums and reaching out blindly, "Where's my hockey stick? Where's the puck? These young whippersnappers think they're so hot on the ice. I'll show them how a real pro plays. Let me at 'em."

"All right, all right," Josh said, knocking Abel over into his pile of pillows. "We all know I'm not a spring chicken."

Josh went to the minibar and retrieved a carton of nog along with two glasses.

"You know he's one of the oldest in the league?" Abel asked me.

"No, I didn't know that. What is the average life expectancy of a hockey player?" I asked seriously while he poured the creamy, cold drinks.

"You'd be surprised," Josh answered without answering and winked at me when he served my drink. "To Christmas," Josh said.

Abel reached for a can of soda he had left by the TV. I raised my glass too.

"To Christmas and to new friends," Josh said.

"To new friends and new beginnings," I added.

"To new friends, new beginnings, and old guys." Abel tipped his head back, finishing off the warm, flat soda in a gulp. "I'm off to bed," he announced suddenly.

"Already?" Josh asked bewildered. "It's only ten o'clock." A distant chime rang out its agreement.

"I need my beauty rest. Good night, you two. Remember, Santa's watching." He laughed and disappeared into the bedroom.

"What was that all about?" I asked, my brain feeling suddenly numb with the thought that Abel suspected his brother and I either were or might become involved.

"Who knows?" Josh answered, unruffled. "He speaks a different language most of the time. So"—he set his cup aside and turned to face me—"have you had a good time so far? Any regrets?"

"No," I gushed. "I mean, yes, I'm having a great time and no, I don't have any regrets."

"Good." He seemed rather self-satisfied. "The Northshore men are generally pretty good hosts."

"I loved the carillon concert tonight." I sat back, feeling the warmth of pleasant company mingling with holiday nostalgia. "I haven't enjoyed a Christmas Eve so much since I was very young. When my mother was still alive . . ."

"I'm glad you enjoyed it. I'm glad you're along," he said. He placed his hand lightly on my knee, but he might as well have set a scalding hot iron on my bare skin, because the nerve-sparking impulses that radiated from there ran over me head to toe and I actually shivered.

"Chilly?" he asked, concerned and already reaching for a quilt.

In no way was I feeling cold, but I accepted the blanket as a convenient and plausible excuse for my trembling. "Thank you."

The clock on the wall filled the silence between us with its ticking. I sat as still as could be, unable and unwilling to move or to wrench my gaze from the sight of him. My breathing was shallow and my hands were shaking. I concentrated briefly on steadying them, then gave up and set the cup of eggnog aside. Leaning forward, I could feel the heat of him radiating like a flame. My brain was paralyzed with desire.

"Josh," I heard myself whisper.

"Yes?" His voice was ragged.

"I . . ." I couldn't think. I didn't want to think. I threw the blanket aside and leaned toward him.

In the space of a twinkling of a Christmas tree light, my arms were wrapped around his shoulders and his hands encircled my waist. I lowered my mouth onto his, hungry for more of that sweet delicacy I had been tempted with the night before. No apologies. Not this time. I knew what I wanted and I wouldn't let some silly notion of professionalism interfere with my personal life. Not now.

"Patricia," he whispered by my ear. "Oh, you're beautiful."

Pent-up longing, like any drug, can cause the host to be-have in ways completely out of character; irrationality and unrestrained emotion take over. I kissed him until I was exhausted, relishing his touch, his warmth, responding to every move he made. When I couldn't take any more, when I knew I had to stop or risk losing command of my senses and plummeting into complete self-indulgence—a luxury I held in close reserve—I pressed away from him, my hands planted firmly on his shoulders and took him in with my eyes only to find myself the subject of his equally enthusiastic admiration.

"I'm so sorry," I stammered. The beautiful numbing fog of desire vanished like a shadow under the sun as thoughts of my student in the next room came crashing in. "I don't know what came over me. I'll be going." I stood and gathered my gifts and purse.

"Don't go," Josh said, a hint of alarm in his voice.

"What?" My mind was still befuddled and my embarrassment level was beginning to climb.

"Don't go," he repeated, more certainly than before.

"I really should," I said, though I made no further move toward the door.

"Don't go." He stood and crossed the space between us in two giant steps.

Toe to toe we gazed at each other. The longing I know must have been heavy in my eyes was mirrored in his. He lowered his mouth over mine again, sweetly, tenderly, gently, slowly. "Don't go."

I stayed until I had no choice but to go. The rosy dawn of Christmas morning touching the window chased away the sensational stupor of the night and broke clear and new on a dizzying prospect: Romance. We spent the night cuddled on the couch watching silly, old Christmas movies with sappy soundtracks and reminiscing about childhood Christmases.

"Good night." I kissed his cheek at the door.

"Good morning," he said, laying his soft lips next to my ear.

"Merry Christmas."

"The merriest."

I walked back to my room with a head full of swirling sensations and a heart lighter than the fluffy snow that was whirling lazily in the air and skittering across my windowpane. Merry Christmas, indeed.

Chapter Eight

"**S**anta Baby" turned out to be a team tradition. Any year when an away game kept the Showboats from home for the holiday, they spent Christmas evening in style. I, of course, was Josh's date, however unofficially, for the merrymaking.

Determined to be everything he remembered from the night before and more, I snipped the tag from Lydia's little delight, the one I swore to Nanna to wear under the green velvet dress. After ascertaining that Abel would not be present at the evening's events, I opted for the black gel-enhanced push-up, which made me shiver and blush alternately and for entirely different reasons. I smoothed on a thin layer of the scent Josh had so enjoyed and pulled Nanna's dance-with-Pat-

Boone dress over my head. It fit like a glove. I realized for the first time in many years that I actually have a desirable figure.

My heels added two inches to my height, my neckline two inches to my bosom. I twisted my hair into as many ringlets as I could manage and piled them on top of my head so that they spilled down just to the nape of my neck where the ruby pendant graced a simple silver chain. Lovely.

Standing before the mirror, I turned this way and that. I have a critical eye. I think it is a job hazard and arises from correcting too many papers. When I look at myself, or anyone else for that matter, the mental red ink pen is uncapped and I begin marking imperfections. Still, I found very little to complain about this evening.

Josh found still less to complain about. When I answered the door, I swear his breath caught. I laughed.

"May I take that as a compliment?" I asked warmly.

"You may, indeed," he said, his eyes taking me in. "You may, indeed." His voice was breathy and he still hadn't looked me in the eye.

"I'll just get my coat," I said, reaching for the red-and-white-striped scarf.

"Allow me." He reached across me and carefully draped the scarf over my shoulders and around my neck, conspicuously leaving my chest uncovered. His hand slid down my arm. His touch conveyed his desire. It was firm, curious. I shivered.

"It's a cold night," he said.

"We'll have to dance close to stay warm," I suggested, turning toward him.

"I brought you something."

"We already exchanged gifts," I said, amazed by the Patricia I saw reflected in his eyes. She was sexy, seductive, sure.

He reached into his pocket and pulled out a little bunch of mistletoe tied with a red ribbon. He held it over my head and kissed me until I knew I would topple off my heels. When he pulled away, I thought I was falling. His arm caught me around the waist.

"Wear it," he said, tucking it into the curls at the crown of my head.

"What if Skywalker or Freddie Kruger get the wrong idea?" I teased.

"They'd just better not." He grinned. "You look beautiful, by the way. If I didn't say so already."

He was rattled. I was thrilled.

"Not in so many words," I teased. "But I got the idea you liked the dress." I smoothed my hands over my hips.

"Yes, I do. The limo should be waiting. Shall we?" He offered his arm.

When we arrived, the restaurant was abuzz with holiday cheer; Christmas in blue and gold never looked so festive. The theme song for the evening could barely be heard overhead as players and friends and even some wives and girlfriends who had been flown in for the occasion laughed and talked, gestured and called. I spotted James "The Fist" and a very lovely woman tucked away in an intimate corner booth, their faces lit by a flickering votive. He whispered in her ear and she blushed.

"Who is that woman with Mr. Allen?" I asked, nodding in their direction.

"That would be Mrs. Allen." Josh laughed at my formality.

"She doesn't call him The Fist, does she?"

"She calls him Jamie," he whispered. "Never call him Jamie."

"What happens if you call him Jamie?"

"You'll meet The Fist." He rubbed his upper arm with an exaggerated grimace on his face and laughed. "Hey, there's Brickman." Josh pointed across the way.

David Brickman waved us over. Josh placed his hand lightly in the small of my back to steer me through the crowd. I noticed Sam Raymond sitting alone and suggested we invite him to join us, but Josh shook his head.

"Join me, Miss Smythe." Brickman pulled a chair out for me.

"Thank you." I took a seat facing the center of the room. The vantage point was perfect. The party was in full swing and beyond the crowd there was a terrific view of the city lights.

"Are you enjoying yourself? Old Northshore treating you right?" Brickman asked me, slugging his teammate in the arm.

"Very nice." I grinned. "I am having a very nice time. Thank you."

"Good." He took a drink.

"Couldn't Sarah join you tonight?" Josh asked.

"Twins have the flu." He shrugged. "Thought about flying back for the day, but from here to there and then there to Seattle tomorrow . . ." He shrugged again.

"You have twins?"

"Girls," he said, reaching for his wallet.

They looked like their father with sandy hair that hung in curls around their round faces.

"Aren't they adorable?" I admired the photo. "How old are they?"

"They'll be eight in May." He beamed. "Having a party with pony rides, balloon animals, the whole nine yards. Sarah's already ordered a cake," he said, shaking his head in amused amazement. "It's shaped like Dorothy's ruby slippers. It's a whole *Wizard of Oz* theme. There are twenty-two or twenty-three kids on the list to invite. Their whole third grade class. Ten are staying the night. It'll be their first sleepover."

"What are their names?" I handed him back his wallet.

"Gabrielle and Serenity." He tucked the treasure back into his hip pocket.

"They're beautiful."

"You should come to the party," he said to Josh. "You, too." He included me. "The more the merrier."

"Sure," Josh said. "Sounds like a good time." He laughed.

I didn't answer. It seemed unnecessary. The assump-

tion had already been made by both of my dinner part-
ners. Eight-year-olds aren't exactly my line of business.
I was already mentally shopping for appropriate gifts.
Maybe matching purses or hats? No. Books. Books with
fancy bookmarks. Or diaries with special heart-shaped
locks that really work.

Josh and Brickman chatted about everything and
nothing and various teammates came by wishing happy
holidays and making predictions about the game in
Seattle. Each one who came by greeted me by name. I
would have felt like one of the guys had it not been for
my figure-hugging emerald-green dress and push-up
gel bra.

"Would you like to dance?" The question came from
behind me.

I turned and found Sam Raymond's face next to mine.

"Oh," I stammered, looking nervously to Josh. Sam
was the only player on the team who I had felt indeci-
sive about. Most of them I had sized up fairly satisfac-
torily, with a little help from Abel and his biographical
sketches on my roster. This one, though, had eluded me.

According to Abel, Sam was an angry man, bitter over
his recent divorce, and not much of a talker. In fact, I had
noticed him several times seating himself just slightly
apart from the rest of the team; I assumed this was his
way of dealing with the pain.

"Sure," I answered softly and stood. "Excuse me,
gentlemen." I winked at Josh as I turned toward the
dance floor. He was half out of his seat. Was he just

being mannerly? Standing when the lady stands? Or, was he trying to rescue me?

Sam's hands were strong as he led me around the dance floor.

"So, Sam, I'm still trying to learn about this sport of yours. You're the goalie?" I asked, knowing full well he was, but hearing Mrs. Trinity's scratchy old voice playing in my memory and admonishing me: "Ladies and gentlemen, at cotillion, the proper partner will make polite conversation as she or he dances."

"Goaltender, yes."

"Have you always been with the Showboats?"

"Started out in Chicago then went to Edmonton. Been with St. Louis three years."

"I've lived in Missouri my whole life. This is my first time in Canada."

As we swept around the dance floor—Sam was a remarkably graceful dancer—my eyes caught Josh standing at the table. I smiled and lifted my hand slightly from Sam's shoulder to wave before I was again facing the other direction. The conversation between my partner and me had waned. One more turn and Josh came into view again. He was striding purposefully across the dance floor. My anticipation of one of those glorious cinematic moments when the hero cuts in on a dance mounted and my heart beat faster.

"May I cut in?" he asked politely, tapping Sam on the shoulder.

Sam stepped aside quickly with a slight nod and disappeared into the dark corners of the restaurant.

"Hi there," I said, allowing myself to be pulled closer than Mrs. Trinity would have deemed proper.

"Hi to you. Listen, didn't anyone ever tell you hockey players are not to be trusted?"

"None of them?" I looked him in the eye.

"None of them." He winked. "Especially not the ones who bring you mistletoe for your hair."

Josh danced divinely. My stamina was no match for his and by the end of our fifth straight song, I was cursing myself for my lack of attention to fitness.

"Ready to sit?" he asked, beaming.

"If you are," I offered bravely.

The coaching staff having arrived, all of the team and any of their families who had flown in for the occasion turned their attention to the platform where the owners, coaches, general manager, and a menagerie of other suits took turns offering kudos and collective wishes for a "Merry Showboats Christmas and a Happy Showboats Year." A handful of astute players lent sincerity to the perfunctory applause by raising their glasses and shouting, "Team!" to which the rest answered "To the team!"

I raised my glass to Josh's. "To the team."

"To you," he returned.

"To new friends," I said, swallowing hard.

"New friends," he whispered, bringing the brim of his glass gently to meet mine.

"What's that I hear?" a booming voice asked from the front. "Why, it's Santa's little helpers!"

"Sorry about this," Josh said, directing me toward our table.

"Sorry for what?"

"This." He gestured toward the double doors at the head of the restaurant just as two lines of young women clad rather scantily in little bright blue dresses trimmed in white fur came through the door, each carrying a bag of gifts.

"I hear you've all been good boys this year," the same booming voice announced. "So, Santa sent some special gifts for you straight from the North Pole. Be sure you show your appreciation."

Catcalls and whistles filled the air.

"They do this with the wives here?" I asked, truly astounded.

Josh nodded sheepishly.

"Maybe I should visit the ladies' room." I started to stand.

"Not a good idea," Brickman interjected.

"Why?"

"We need you here for protection." His sincerity made me laugh.

"You're on your own." I winked and slipped out of my chair, edging toward the back of the room as quickly and discreetly as possible as the strobe light pumped and the breathy singing voice of a Madonna lookalike echoed over the crowd.

Leaning against the wall, I watched as Josh and Brickman, apparently the two curmudgeons in this band of hedonists, tried to retain a sense of decorum at the center of the show. It was all over, however, when not one, not two, but three of the voluptuous elfettes converged at their table, presents in hand and pressing cherry-red, high-glossed lips against their burning faces. I could see Josh's wide eyes narrowing as he spotted me over the bare shoulders of some twenty-year-old whose present pose undoubtedly left little to the imagination. His one free hand beckoned, but I stood, resolute, and very amused. Poor Brickman gave up altogether and paid for his gift with the requisite peck on the cheek.

I could see the agony mounting in Josh's face. His determination was admirable, but when the fun was over it was over. What could possibly have caused me to abandon all senses, I don't know, but I strode back across the room as quickly as my straight skirt and tall heels would allow, tapped the flirty young thing on her alabaster shoulder, smiled sweetly as she stood to face me, leaned in and planted one firm kiss square on her pink, sparkling cheek. The crowd went wild, as they say. I held out my hand to accept the gift on Josh's behalf before she skipped off on her merry way.

"What was that all about?" Brickman was impressed.

"Defending my territory." I winked at Brickman as I offered the gift to Josh.

"No, keep it. You earned that one," he said.

Brickman threw his head back and laughed a rich, genuine laugh. "To the team,"

"To the team," I agreed.

"What was it like?" Josh asked, a mischievous glint in his eye.

I licked my lips in consideration. "She tasted like peanuts."

"So did mine!" Brickman hooted.

"Good thing I didn't kiss her," Josh said solemnly. "I'm allergic."

The peak of the celebration having passed, Josh and I indulged in one last slow dance before excusing ourselves and heading back to the hotel.

"You're a wonderful dancer. Where did you learn?"

"I had a coach once who insisted that learning to dance would help you maintain control on the ice."

"I thought how graceful you look out there. I mean, when you're not smashing some guy against the wall."

"Boards," he corrected.

"Boards. It's very much a paradox, isn't it? Hockey? It's refinement and violence combined."

"Do you enjoy it?" He turned his eyes to me, searching mine for affirmation.

"The game? Or you in the game?" I teased.

"Both."

"Yes. Both."

"Thanks for saving me tonight."

"Sometimes a girl's gotta do what a girl's gotta do."

"Defending her territory?" he prodded.

I couldn't speak. Was he making fun? Challenging me? What? I bravely locked eyes with his. I would force him into making the next move.

"You were great tonight," he said earnestly.

"I'm great every night." I forced a sardonic laugh.

"I'll bet you are," he said, his eyes never leaving my face, not for an instant, not even when the driver pulled to the curb and opened the door, not even when he took my hand to help me out of the car.

When Josh turned to walk away, leaving me standing in the open door of my room, aching for him, I knew he had my features by memory and he would be seeing me in his dreams.

Chapter Nine

Seattle was rainy. Big surprise. Abel's excitement was not to be contained. The Aerosmith concert was within reach and Josh had agreed to fly in Kyle, the mute boy from the mall, so that Abel wouldn't have to go to the "jamminest concert ever" with his older brother.

In the hours preceding the concert, however, my charge and I tore into *Le Morte d'Artur*. The holiday had slammed our studies into the boards, but now it was time to resume play. The hotel in Seattle was much like the one in Toronto and, again, Abel and I found a quiet coffee shop in the lobby where we were able to discuss the king of the great legends, his knights, his ladies, his life, his death, and his mythical transport across the River Styx, all while savoring the creamy, sugary, and aromatic coffee drinks this town was famous for.

Abel amazed me. This young man, whose sole purpose in St. Louis had seemed to be taking up space in an already crowded classroom, seemed to thrive with one-on-one instruction. He was becoming more inquisitive and less surly. I enjoyed our discussions. Abel was showing signs of self-assurance in his answers, able to talk about how the things of literature related to his own life or how this or that story or poem related to another we'd read. Seeing this side of him really did revive in me my teacher's heart.

"Good work," I said, closing the book. "We're getting close, Abel. Are you going to be ready for your mid-term exam?"

"I think so." He shrugged and downed the thick remains of his drink. "It's multiple choice, right?"

"Not on your life." I frowned. "Short answer and essay."

"When?"

"We still need to do Margery Kempe. After that, we're ready. Why don't we plan for . . ." I consulted my calendar. "We're due in Chicago in a couple of days. How about we do it there?"

"Great."

"There's a lengthy excerpt in your anthology. Read it and the poem "A Valediction Forbidding Mourning." We'll see how we can tie the two together."

"Okay." his answer was soft and his eyes downcast. His mind seemed a million miles away. The maturing young man I had enjoyed teaching only a few minutes earlier withdrew and that other Abel re-emerged. I was sad to see him go but felt confident he'd be back.

"Enjoy the concert tonight," I offered. "What time does Kyle's flight get in?"

"Three. I'm taking a cab to the airport to meet him. We're gonna grab a pizza before the concert."

"Be careful. I hate the idea of you roaming around a strange city like this."

"I'm eighteen, Miss Smythe," he said as if that should put to rest any reservations.

"Yes"—I raised an eyebrow—"remember that."

"Catch you later," he said, ignoring my advice with the ease of the practiced.

"Bye." I sat back to reread some of the assignment I had just made for Abel. My coffee had turned cold.

The last day of the calendar year is a mystery to me. I hate the idea that I am so ready to be shed of the previous months of my life. It smacks of failure. On the other hand, the prospect of the coming year is always bright. Somehow I manage to rekindle the hopes and dreams that have gone unfulfilled to this point and step into the new year resolved to make things happen.

Usually, New Year's Eve finds me having dinner with a group of friends and then attending a party at the Calhoun's sprawling, suburban home, which is, inevitably, still decorated for Christmas, or begging off and spending the evening at home with Dick Clark on the television while I pack away my own holiday decorations. This year, however, I had a to-do to do. The team was celebrating in style in some swanky restaurant atop a tower. I had been asked to accompany three different Showboats players, but had accepted the invitation of one, Mr. Northshore.

Finishing with Abel early in the afternoon gave me time to hunt down a new dress for the occasion, so I quickly dropped off my English teacher's bag of tricks in my room, pulled on a raincoat and hit the streets of Seattle in search of something innocently seductive and probably in black. Seven dress shops and three shoe stores later, after trying six sweetly sexy dresses and four pairs of heels up to four inches tall, I selected one simple but classy clutch and plucked a matching necklace and earring set from a display on my way to the register. I returned to the hotel with three shopping bags, ready to forgo the whole evening in favor of a long, hot bubble bath, a cheese pizza delivered to the room and a Doris Day and Rock Hudson marathon.

The bubble bath turned out to be just what I needed. Warm ripples coursed across my chilled skin and the slight tickle of bursting jasmine and white tea-scented bubbles put me in the right frame of mind to slip into the black, scoop-necked, knee-skimming dress with the deep red velvet trim at the neckline, wrists, and hem. My old friend Roberta at Lydia's again proved her expertise and the red sateen strapless made its debut.

I hate nylons. In my profession, trousers are perfectly acceptable and, thus, I have an abundance of socks and knee-high tights. The few pairs of hosiery I do own are opaque and reserved for my long corduroy and tweed winter skirts. However, in the spirit of celebration, and in a moment of decadence and self-confidence, I had purchased a pair of sheer, black, lace-topped, thigh-high silk stockings. At five minutes to eight, I turned around in front of the full-length mirror, feeling very girly and very anxious about the evening. Butterflies swarmed in my stomach and I felt faint when Josh's knock came at the door. I just knew I would slip in my new heels while on the dance floor and fall out of my shoes at best, or out of my dress at worst.

Anxious about my New Year's Eve with Josh, I had taken the now fairly tattered *Girl's Guide* to the tub and read a chapter on the much debated history of the sport and another on what could be termed iconic players. As much as I hated to admit it, I had begun rather enjoying the games. Watching for Josh to take his shift was part of it, but even when he wasn't on the ice there was a thrill in the thrust of the game. I found myself as enthralled as ever I was in a piece of beautifully written prose or verse. I couldn't take my eyes from the motion of players on the ice, which was vaguely reminiscent of the tide coming in and going out again: An indescribable gracefulness met perfectly with an irrepressible force coming from somewhere beneath; it was orchestrated yet surprising.

"Wow," he said as he extended a single rose, yellow with an orange vein.

"Thank you. I love yellow roses."

"You seemed the kind of girl who might."

"What sort of girl is that?" I asked mischievously, filling a glass with water for the rose.

A smile broke over his face. He had no answer. I laughed.

"Are you ready?"

"Just let me grab my bag and a wrap. Is it still raining?"

"Buckets." He helped me on with my coat.

The city lights were a kaleidoscope through the rivulets racing down the floor-to-ceiling windows. We sat, agreeably quiet, at our intimate corner table for two and watched nature's display roll across the sky. I stole glances at him and he stole glances at me. If, by chance, our eyes met over the glow of the softly burning votive between us, we smiled, lowered our eyes, and sipped our wine, nervous as two teenagers on their first date.

Had I noticed before how fine his features were? His jawline a study in geometry, his eyes two circles cut from a Monet.

"Where are you tonight?" he asked, as if reading my mind.

"I was reading that the actual beginnings of this game of yours are somewhat questionable?" My senses refused to come completely back to me, the words sounded like a dream echo.

Josh chuckled. "There is some debate."

"What are your thoughts?"

"My thoughts?" He raised his eyebrows.

"Yes."

"Oh, Miss Smythe, my thoughts have absolutely nothing to do with hockey tonight."

He reached his hand across the table, his upturned fingers beckoned. I placed my hand lightly in his; he raised it to his lips, turning it palm up, and pressing a firm kiss at its center. I closed my fingers over it. He leaned across the table.

"I'm not sorry," he said.

"I'm not sorry either."

He led me to the dance floor and held me close. I felt brave. I lifted my face to his and kissed him. A clever clarinetist was playing "Misty."

"Happy New Year," he said by my ear as someone started counting down to midnight.

"The happiest," I answered as a shout went up and the band played "Auld Lang Syne." He kissed me again and I fell in love at that very moment.

The incessant knocking on my door mingled with the beating of my heart in a dream shaped by a dance, a kiss, and a midnight toast; it wasn't until I heard my name called sharply from without that I was able to shake off the delightfully drowsy delirium and open the door to the new year.

"Yes?" I asked, unable to focus well enough to see through the peep hole.

"Patricia, it's me," Josh said, knocking again even more deliberately. "Abel's missing."

"What?" I pulled my robe around me and opened the

door for him, horrified at the thought of what I must look like.

"Abel's missing," he repeated, entering quickly and walking straight to the window as if he might spot him.

"Are you sure?" I asked, quickly checking my breath while his back was turned and reaching for a ponytail holder.

"He never came home last night," he said without taking his eyes from the window.

"What about Kyle?"

"No. Neither one of them has been back to the room since they left yesterday for pizza before the concert."

"Have you called anyone?" I asked, trying desperately to dislodge that sleepy senselessness.

"I talked to the night manager downstairs and to security. They said Abel and Kyle never came through last night. The head of security is trying to get in touch with the guys who worked the concert last night to see if any of them remember seeing the two of them there." He turned to face me and his cell phone rang, as if on cue. "Josh Northshore."

I watched anguish and worry settle on his beautiful face like ash coming to rest. His voice was older, strained.

"What did they say?" I asked as he hung up.

"One of the security guys remembers seeing the two of them at the concert. He said they went out about twenty minutes before the concert ended and he doesn't remember seeing them come back in."

"Were there security cameras on the parking lot or

outside the box office?" My thoughts were quickly clarifying as the adrenaline started to course through me.

"They're checking it out to see if they can get a time and maybe a direction."

"Did you try Abel's phone?"

"Shut off."

"What about Kyle's?"

"Same."

"Have you called the police?"

"I reported it."

"And?"

"They're not considered missing until twenty-four hours have passed, but they took a description and they'll be on the lookout for them in the meantime."

"What about Kyle's parents?"

"I haven't called yet."

"Shouldn't you?"

"Yeah," he said in a near whisper.

"Sit down," I said, pointing to my rumpled and probably still warm bed.

He complied.

"What should I do?" He looked at me, his eyes pleading, searching for an answer.

"Give me the number. I'll call his mother and explain. Then"—the thoughts were quickly jumbling again—"then, I'll get dressed, we'll go downstairs, get a seat by the windows in the restaurant so we can see the entrance to the hotel, have a little breakfast and figure it out from there. Okay?"

"Okay," he agreed softly and relinquished his phone.

I scrolled through his numbers without any qualms, not seeing anything as I searched for Kyle's number. I dialed. Josh watched me closely as if expecting me to spontaneously combust when Kyle's mother answered. I turned away. He was making me even more nervous.

One frantic mother in St. Louis and a perfectly hand-some, completely-in-love-with-me, but too-over-the-edge-to-do-anything-about-it hockey player in Seattle . . . what more could a girl want on New Year's Day? Josh paced window to door and back again while I brushed my teeth and got changed. When I emerged from the fogged-over bathroom, I found him standing again at the window drumming his fingers on the frosted glass.

"Come on," I said, looping my arm through his. "I'll buy you breakfast."

The front doors to the hotel must have opened a hun-dred and fifty times while we sat nursing coffees and picking at pastries, turning our heads at the sound of every young man's voice echoing in the lobby and start-ing every time the doorman admitted someone.

"I'm sure he's fine," I said, reaching across to pat his hand.

"Yeah," he said, unconvinced.

"This isn't like him?"

"No." He shook his head. "Not for a long time."

"How long?"

"He ran away once when he was in eighth grade."

"Ah, the middle school years. Hell on everyone. Where did he go?"

"He went to Detroit."

"Why Detroit?"

"That's where our mother was at the time. In a facility there. He ran away to see her."

"How long before you found him?"

"He made it there in a week, and after about three days someone there got the idea that a kid this age probably shouldn't be showing up alone all the time. I got a call from the head nurse, just checking . . ."

"What happened?"

"They kept him until I could get there. Brought him home. We fought for weeks. I was afraid every time I had to go out. That's when I hired Mrs. Flannery to stay on. She might not be able to keep him from getting away, but she's at least another set of eyes."

"But, that was five years ago. Why would he do this now? I mean, things seem to be going so well. We were just talking about his mid-term exam. He's up to his last reading and he'll graduate in May. Why would he take off now?"

"I don't know." Josh sighed and put his head in his hands.

The doors opened again and a young couple entered. I watched them cross the lobby to the front desk. I was briefly distracted and envious. Just a few hours ago, I had the full attention of a desirous man; the same man sat across from me now, agonizing in a private hell and only vaguely cognizant of my presence.

"You sure he didn't leave a note or anything?"

"No," he said.

"I think I'll check my e-mail," I said, standing. "There's a computer right over there." I pointed to a desk just a few yards away. I was desperate for a break in the tension.

"Okay." Josh said and nodded.

My fingers trembled as I typed in my password. I clasped my hands in my lap to try and still them as the screen came up. Two messages. Nanna's New Year's note read:

> *Patty, I hope midnight finds you wrapped in a dream and the New Year brings with it a lifetime supply of romance. Love and kisses, Nanna.*

Abel's last e-mail was timed at 4:17 P.M. the day before. The subject line was "Tennyson's Torment" and there was an attachment.

> *Miss Smythe, I'm attaching the essay you assigned for* The Lady of Shallot. *Hope it's any good. Thnx, Abe.*

A self-satisfied smile emerged. Success. Not only had my student met the challenge of a time-intensified curriculum, he had connected with a classic poem he had claimed as his own. I glanced back at Josh, who had turned toward the window and seemed no better or worse for my momentary absence. I opened the attachment:

Tennyson's poem, The Lady of Shallot, *despite its age, is an important study for modern man, whose life is as rife with isolation and pain as the lady's, whose courageous confrontation of this curse brought her both death and recognition.*

"Wow, Abel, that's really good," I said aloud. I let my eyes scan the pages. Isolation. Despair. Pain. A typical reading of a classical piece. Then, I saw something new. A spark of insight, personal and profound:

Her salvation, her rescue, was not within her own reach. Rather, it was within the reach of those who marched by her in the daily parade of commerce and camaraderie. They could have saved her, if only they would. A single glance, a meeting of eyes in the glass, would have let her know she wasn't truly alone (because none of us are ever truly alone in this life). The curse is really on those who fail to recognize the importance of one life touching another.

> *God, in his mercy lend them grace*
> *Who fail to reach across the space*
> *To meet another face to face*

And so confine her to the place
Where reason has lost its crucial race . . .
   The Lady of Shallot.

"Josh!" I called across the lobby and waved wildly.

"What is it?" he asked, wild-eyed.

"Where is your mother now?"

"My mother?"

"Yes. Where is she now?"

"Oregon."

"That's where he's gone. I'm sure of it."

"Did he say so?" He peered at the essay on the screen and saw nothing to substantiate my assertion.

"I'm sure that's where he's gone. Josh"—I reached up and tenderly turned his face until our eyes met—"I'm sure."

It was late that night when a softer, almost timid knock woke me from a disturbing dream. I dreamt I was tangled in a red-and-white-striped rope. I couldn't move. I was calling for help but no one could hear me. Then, as can happen only in a dream, I was suddenly riding along in Josh's Mustang. We were chatting about something unimportant when I noticed headlights in our lane. I screamed. The next thing I knew, I was watching them lower my mother's coffin into the ground, only, instead of a rose, I threw a handful of papers into the grave after her. They fluttered in the wind before sinking below ground level and coming to rest. The knocking at my door echoed my heart beating in my ears as I awoke, startled.

"Yes?" I called, trying to shake away the disturbing images and the sense of dread which accompanied them.

"Patricia, it's Josh," he almost whispered.

"Coming." I hurried to the door without bothering to check my appearance as I passed the mirror.

At my insistence, Josh had phoned the home where his mother was a resident. The desk clerk reported that a young man had come to visit Mrs. Northshore earlier that morning, but had stayed only a little while, maybe half an hour or so. He had signed in under the name of Josiah Northshore, but the clerk had overheard him introducing himself to Mrs. Northshore as Abel. When asked, Mrs. Northshore apparently had no recollection of her morning visitor and became rather aggitated when questioned further.

While I phoned the airport and the bus terminals, Josh talked Kyle's mother out of taking an afternoon flight to Washington. A Greyhound worker recalled seeing two young men who fit my rather generic description; in fact, they were waiting for their bus even as we spoke. She paged Abel Northshore for an emergency phone call. I handed the phone to Josh whose face registered a spectrum of emotion from fear to relief to anger in a span of only a few seconds.

"No need. Sit tight. I'll be there as quick as I can," Josh said before hanging up. "They had only enough money for one ticket home. Since Kyle's flight leaves this afternoon, he was going to take the bus and Abel was going to stay at the terminal until Kyle got here to ask me to call with my credit card number so he could get aboard a later bus."

"Do you want me to go along?" I asked, feeling both hopeful that he would want my company and apprehensive that I would be intruding into a family matter.

"Thanks for offering, but it's probably better if I go this one alone. Do you understand?"

"Absolutely," I said, patting him on the arm and giving him a smile, which I hoped conveyed my sympathy and my hope that things would be back to where we had left off very soon. "Go. Just let me know when you get back. Okay?"

"Thanks, Patricia," he said, giving me a quick, gentle kiss on the cheek.

The day stretched out long in front of me. I reread Abel's essay a couple of times, absorbing its tenor and searching for quiet revelations of this young man on the brink of adulthood and carrying with him a heavy load of fear and anxiety, guilt and frustration. I put it aside and tried to write, but my thoughts were too jumbled. The Northshores' life had become enmeshed with mine; even my dreams were confused. This was not a good time to soul search. I decided to go shopping while I waited for word on Abel.

I ventured as far as a secondhand book shop down the block. I'm a goner when I find a secondhand book shop. Kiss at least two hours good-bye. I love the familiar smell of old paper and binding glue. The musty perfume in this little shop, Recycled Reads, was intensified by the rain.

"Good morning," said the college-aged girl perched behind the counter. "Help you find anything?"

"No, I'm just browsing. Thanks." I waved congenially before disappearing into the towering stacks which were bursting at the seams with paperbacks of all kinds. I breathed in deeply and felt a much desired calmness settle over my face, neck, shoulders and chest. Books. My drug of choice.

I picked up a copy of Mary Shelley's *Frankenstein* knowing full well my library at home already contained two editions of the same book, one from my college lit course and one I found later on with a much more appealing cover. This one, however, was marked up. Someone named Sage Whitelaw, whose name was scrawled on the inside cover, had studied this classic and made his or her notes in the margins throughout. I fancied I could determine Sage's gender based on the comments written inside. The used bookstores I know wouldn't normally accept something like this for resale, but I treasure the volumes which bear the literal mark of some former reader's experiences with the text. I am myself a page-marker-upper. I also decided on a volume of Tennyson's poems, nicely bound and costing too much, for a graduation gift for Abel, and a copy of *Beowulf* with beautifully illuminated text, costing way too much, for Josh.

Waiting at the register, a display of hand-beaded bookmarks caught my eye. At $5 apiece, I decided to surprise my literacy group. Each bookmark boasted a colorful pattern and a little engraved charm. Digging through them while the pretty student grinned at me over the top of her book, *Dairy Devils: Confronting the Milk Industry,* I was fortunate enough to find each member's initials—although, I had to dig through twice to find enough S's: Sam, Stu, Sharon, and Sara.

"This it?" the young one asked, laying aside her ponderous read to ring my purchase.

"It had better be." I smiled, watching the numbers on the display screen and trying to read her shirt without looking like I was staring at her chest. It said, FAIR TRADE OR NO TRADE! and had a Web address across the bottom. I wondered if it was her own site.

She paused briefly before ringing up the *Frankenstein.* The slightest hint of a smile lifted the corners of her mouth. I thought she must be familiar with the story.

The rain had let up considerably and I considered a quaint café for a light lunch, but I was chilly and there were too many content-looking people eating soup and smiling. I was afraid the worry that had met up with me again just outside the door of the bookshop might spoil my mood, so I settled for room service and a run of television classics from the 50s, 60s and 70s. Finally, as twilight began to close in, I pulled the drapes and phoned Nanna.

"How are you, Patty? I haven't heard from you for several days. Are you having a good time?"

"I'm having a very good time, Nanna." I was determined not to let this momentary blip ruin the entire trip. "A very good time. How's Mr. O'Malley?"

"You mean Mr. Stevenson?"

"Do I?"

"Yes, Mr. Stevenson."

"What happened to Mr. O'Malley?"

"Mr. O'Malley refused to dance with me. Mr. Stevenson is Fred Astair."

"Oh, so how's Mr. Stevenson?"

"Gorgeous." I could actually hear her smiling.

"Really?"

"Yes. He took me out New Year's Eve. We went dancing and ate Thai food. My stomach's just recovering. Oh, but did we have fun!"

"Good. I'm glad. Are you going out again soon?"

"Tonight. We're going to a poetry reading at the university. He still teaches a class, you know."

"What kind of a class?"

"Art appreciation. He's asked me to pose for him." Her tone became evocative.

"Pose?"

"Yes, pose. Why is that so outrageous?"

"It just surprises me, that's all."

"Why?" She laughed. "It's art, dear. Haven't you ever noticed the best portraits show all the wrinkles and lines? Well, my portrait should be a real doozie."

Sometime after my second bag of microwavable pop-corn and third "Brady Bunch" episode, I fell asleep. I had hoped Josh would call just to let me know that they were all safe and sound, but he hadn't. I wondered what the drive back to Seattle would be like for them. I hoped that they were able to be calm; I hoped Josh didn't come down too hard on his brother.

The soft tapping on the door became more intense. Normally, being awakened suddenly makes me grumpy, but I was so relieved to see Josh standing there.

"Come in." I stepped aside.

"Only for a minute," he said. "I need to get back to business, if you know what I mean."

"Of course." I understood, but was disappointed nonetheless. "What about your game tonight?"

"I've been excused tonight. Family crisis and all." He sat on the bed looking a far different person than he had in that same setting this morning. He looked older, weary, sad.

I sat beside him. He smiled a little. I kissed his cheek and he turned toward me, crushing me in his embrace. "Thank you," he kept saying, but I don't think he was talking to me.

"He's okay?" I finally asked.

"Yeah." He straightened and ran his hand over his face. "He's grounded forever but he's okay."

"I'm glad."

"Look, Patricia, I'm going to be asking the managers for the next two games off. Going to take Abel on back to St. Louis and spend a few days working all this out before school starts. I don't want any leftover trauma messing up what he's worked on with you over break. I want him to go into his last semester ready to work hard. He said you were going to give him his mid-term exam in Chicago. Is he ready now? Could he take it tomorrow on the flight home?"

"Sure." This seemed an extreme reaction to me but it was his decision to make. "He can finish reading Margery Kempe and just take that part cold."

"Good." He stood. "He'll read it tonight. We'll leave for the airport tomorrow morning at eight. Can you be ready then?"

"Yes," I said, my heart sinking.

"Thanks, Patricia, for everything."

"You're welcome." I was still sitting on the bed as he stood at the threshold. "I guess I'll see you in the morning, then," I added, the heaviness of the day taking its toll on us all. "Good night." I stood.

"Good night," he said, pulling the door behind him.

I sank back to the bed. Tears puddled in my eyes. I was so relieved to hear Abel was safe. Everything would work out fine. He would pass his mid-term and start the second semester with a clean slate. That had been the goal of the trip, its sole purpose really. Still, my heart ached at the thought that the end of the trip might also mean the end of a budding romance.

A budding romance. At my age, that really was a joke. Not much in my life could be considered budding. Then, look at Nanna. She's seventy-six years old for Pete's sake and she's in a budding romance. The poets speak of the bloom of youth; maybe the poets are wrong.

I looked at myself in the mirror—really scrutinized my reflection. I looked different to myself than I had a week ago. Is that what hope does? Changes a person's visage only slightly, yet perceptibly? Had Josh noticed the change? My cheeks were a little rosier. My eyes had a light behind them which I hadn't ever seen before. Could all of this co-exist with disappointment? Not for long. In fact, I saw it fading away like woodsmoke vanishing on a breezy autumn day. I hung the hotel bathrobe over the glass and started packing. I purposely left behind the bottle of Chai lotion.

Chapter Ten

Abel aced his exam. He finished it midway between Seattle and St. Louis. I graded it on the second leg of the trip and handed it back to him along with a note, which read:

You did it! Congratulations, Graduate-to-Be.

His shy and quiet, "Thank you," were about the only words spoken on the entire trip. I shook his hand and whispered back, "Yeah." He smiled weakly and turned his eyes back to the prized exam paper on his lap.

I gave Josh a quick thumbs up as I passed and he wiped his brow dramatically. I hesitated, hoping he would pat the seat beside him, beckon me down for a quick kiss, say, "Thank you," or something. Instead, he turned to look out the window. I decided then and there that I wouldn't allow myself any more carefree fantasies about what might be between us. There was too much in the way right now and though I understood his distraction, I did feel a little injured. Pride, I suppose, does that.

When we landed at Lambert, I thanked Josh for a great time and shook his hand to eliminate any conflict he might be feeling in regard to me. His smile was small but grateful. I wanted so much to kiss his cheek, to tell him that the trip had been wonderful, memorable; I wanted to tell him our friendship was an unexpected delight and I hoped we'd see each other again. Soon. Instead, I turned on my heels and walked as quickly and purposefully as I possibly could toward the row of taxis waiting outside.

"See you next semester," I called to Abel and feigned a carefree wave.

"Don't you want a ride?" Abel shouted after me.

"No, thanks. Enjoy the rest of your break." I closed the door on the cab and busied myself with putting on my mittens, refusing to look up as we passed the Northshore brothers standing on the curb. It was simply too hard driving away.

When the taxi pulled into my driveway, I was relieved not to find Nanna's red Land Rover parked and Bitsy tied to my tree. She had promised to take in the mail while I was gone and I fully expected her impeccable timing to put her there just as I pulled in. At least

I might have an hour or so before she showed up to get myself together and come up with a good story as to why I was back so soon. I didn't feel the need to explain the ins and outs, or at least what I understood to be the ins and outs, of the Northshore saga to Nanna, nor did I want her to think that I had what she would term "chickened out" on the trip. No, Nanna would never know that I had even been within spitting distance of a romance with Josh. The best thing would be for her to think that I am just such a whiz-kid at my job that we simply finished early and there was no need to stay on, which, in essence, turned out to be true. Abel had earned his passing grade and had proven himself to be a careful reader, a skilled analyzer, a practiced writer and effective communicator. He had passed his mid-term exam. What further purpose could I have served?

I told myself it was good to be home as I stepped up to my front porch, but my heart knew I lied and called me on it by sending a deep sigh and a vague headache my way as soon as I turned the key in the lock. Everything was just as I'd left it. There was a tree to take down and decorations to put away; there were groceries to be bought and laundry to do. There was more than enough to keep me occupied until school resumed next week. Besides, there were journal entries to be written, promising readers to assist, lessons to plan, bookstores to be visited and fancy coffees to be drunk. There was plenty to occupy the time.

I turned on all the lights in the room and opened the

blinds. It was time to breathe some life into this place and to forget that for a split-second along the dull, gray continuum that is my life, there had been at least the hope of something new.

I dragged my luggage down the hallway and hefted it onto the bed, which I had left unmade—I truly am a slob sometimes. I noticed the used paperback I'd picked up a few weeks earlier opened and turned face down on the chair. I had really been enjoying the silly plotline before Josh walked into my classroom and took over my life. *Took over my life? Is that really what had happened?*

"Errrr," I growled at myself in frustration and threw open the lid to my case. I tossed almost everything into the hamper, but the treasures from Lydia's went into the trash. I stashed the unopened bottles of Asian Mystery and Tiger Lily lotions at the back of my sock drawer. "Nanna likes them? She'll get them back for her birthday," I said, slamming the drawer shut a little too hard and rocking the porcelain figurine of a mother and daughter in an embrace, which I had purchased in a mood of self-pity one year on the anniversary of my mother's death. It toppled. I reached out to grab it, but instead knocked it back toward the dresser. There was a sickening cracking sound before it came to rest.

My heart pounded and I reached out to see how much damage had been done. A tiny, tiny crack trailed along the daughter's dress. It wasn't shattered. It wasn't even broken, just slightly damaged.

"That's okay. It just gives it character," I said aloud, wishing for the reassuring sound of a human voice, even if it was my own. I placed the treasure back on top of the dresser and silently vowed to be more careful and not let my anger get the best of me.

Anger? Is that what I am feeling? You bet it was. I was mad. I mean, really mad. Who did this Northshore character think he was anyway? First of all, what man in his right mind asks a public schoolteacher to give up her vacation, come along on a trip with a bunch of strange men, and give private lessons to his brother who didn't care enough about his grades to pass class in the first place? An egotist, that's who. And, who was he to presume to lead me down the path of some ridiculous romance when he knew good and well it would end as soon as the plane touched down in St. Louis? How would he even know whether I'm a yellow rose kind of girl or not? I might be a . . . a . . . a . . . what? I might be a gardenia girl! Or, a lily girl! Or I might not even like flowers at all! He doesn't know me. So he majored in Romantic literature? So he has a dog named Grendel? So what? He's a hockey player, for heaven's sake. A hockey player! He's nobody to me. His brother is a nice but mixed up kid who let himself get too far behind in his work and needed a little extra help. He did what he needed to do to arrange things to his own benefit. People do that. It's no surprise. I'm not a fool. Why didn't I see it coming?

I sat on the bed and held the pillow close. Then, I kicked the cases to the floor, scooched down under the rumpled covers, turned my face into the pillow and howled. I howled for a good long time and then I stopped. I sat up, wiped my eyes and reached for the phone. Josh's business card still lay next to my alarm clock. I dialed. I hung up. I kicked my legs in a childish tantrum and then I scooched down under the covers again and cried some more.

When the police cars pulled into my driveway at 5:00, I thought someone must have died. I raced to the front door and stubbed my toe on the ottoman. Before the bell rang, I jerked open the door. Two officers stood on my porch looking perplexed. Nanna and Bitsy were right behind them in matching blue sweaters with sequined fireworks displays and LET THE BALL DROP! emblazoned across the front. Nanna was also wearing pink and purple toe socks and a pair of Dr. Scholls' wooden-soled sandals from about 1976.

"What's wrong?" I asked Nanna.

"Patty?"

"Do you know this woman?" one of the officers asked my grandmother.

"This is my granddaughter," she said, stepping front and center.

"The one who owns the house?" The second officer smirked.

"What are you doing here? You're supposed to be in Seattle. Or was it Chicago?"

"Is everything all right?" the first officer asked me. "The house is secure? No intruders?"

"Everything's fine. I'm afraid I'm a little confused, though."

"Your lights were on and the front door wasn't locked when I turned the knob. I thought about getting the tire iron from the Land Rover and coming in anyway, but Bitsy was acting anxious, so I thought I should just call the police. What are you doing home?" Her eyes narrowed. "You had a fling with the hockey player and now you're feeling guilty because of his brother, so you came home early. You chickened out, didn't you? I knew it." She shook her head, already convinced of the truth of her fictional account. "I knew it. I knew it. I knew it. Chickened out."

"Well, if everything's okay, we'll be on our way," the first officer said, smiling at me and nodding as if he suspected this wasn't the first or the last time I'd have to deal with my insane old grandmother's chaos-causing confusion.

"Thank you." I smiled weakly. "Nanna, come in. It's cold out here."

"Thank you, officers," she said, very regally.

"Not at all," they said in unison.

"Happy New Year," I offered apologetically.

Nanna stepped into the warmth, the excitement of the afternoon's events revealing itself in incessant chatter. I stood in the doorway watching the officers get back into their car, laughing uproariously. Bitsy joined me and danced on her hind feet until I picked her up.

"Hello, Bitsy. How are you?" I asked her in my best baby talk voice. "How's Bitsy?" I was rewarded with a plentiful supply of wet, cold doggy kisses on my nose and eyelids.

"So, what happened?" Nanna sat in my favorite chair, put her feet on the ottoman, and pulled a quilt across her lap—she was there for the duration.

"Nothing so tawdry as the scenario you just invented. And thank you, by the way, for leading the kind officers to believe I'm tramping around with some hockey player."

"And his brother." Nanna's eyes glinted with the wicked realization that her conjecture could have been construed in a completely different way. "What did happen, then?"

"Abel turned out to be a dedicated student and we finished early. There," I said, sitting down and shrugging lightly. "That's the story. So, what's new with you? Posed for any artistic studies lately?" I couldn't help adding a sarcastic snort.

"As a matter of fact"—she hesitated—"Mr. O'Malley called. It seems he's willing to take up dancing if I'll come back and be his sweetie pie again. So, Mr. Stevenson is just going to have to find another tomato." Her laugh proved her positively irredeemable.

"Tomato?"

"Never mind." Nanna shook her head, despairing of me altogether. "So, what about the hockey player?"

"What about him?" I shrugged again, trying with all my might to disguise the irritation I was feeling at the mention of Josh.

"Yes"—she leaned toward me—"what about him?" Her tone was leading. I wasn't fooling anyone.

"He flew back with us this morning. Needed to take care of some business with Abel. We said good-bye at the airport. I suppose he'll be back on the ice by next week."

"And he'll be calling you?"

"Why would he do that?" I blinked innocently.

"Hmmm." Nanna sat back completely dissatisfied with the information she'd been able to obtain, but willing to wait for the timid deer to come a little closer before making any further moves. "So, what do you want to do about dinner?"

"Actually, Nanna, I'm really tired. I thought I'd just open a can of soup and fall into bed early tonight." I stood, hoping the hint would be taken.

"Sure, Patty. You probably need your rest what with all those books and papers and time zones. Call me tomorrow. Okay?"

"Sure, Nanna. Thanks for taking care of the house while I was gone."

"You're welcome. Come on Bitsy. Good night."

I slept only intermittently that night and the next. By the time midweek rolled around, I had worked up enough personal courage to actually shower and put on regular clothes. Looking at myself in the mirror, I would have sworn I'd aged in the past two days. I put on a little more makeup, pulled on my Showboats sweatshirt—strictly as a show of bravado—my striped gloves, scarf *and* hat, and drove to the LaFayette Community Church where the noontime group—not mine—known as the Brown Bag Bunch was having a session on business reading. Hillary, the Brown Bagger's coach and volunteer coordinator for the program, would be there. She could fill me in on what had gone on in my absence. I'd missed a whopping two sessions with my group. Also, she'd know I was available to resume my duties this week instead of next.

"Patricia! How are you?" Hillary greeted me with a hug. "How was your trip?"

"Good. It was good." I felt a twinge of guilt but reminded myself that I had enjoyed the trip up until the very end. "Glad to be back, though."

"Great! You're ready to be back in the saddle, then?"

"Sure am."

"Well, they'll be glad to have you back. They missed you."

It was good to be missed. We chatted only briefly because Hillary needed to get back to the Brown Baggers. I waved and exited through a side door. Sitting in the car, I looked up at the steeple. The winter sun glinted off the copper sheets, showing off its depth. Across the street, a large park had attracted a few hearty joggers whose desire to be fit was stronger than the desire to be warm. I breathed in the fresh air and feeling refreshed, I headed for the coffee shop. There was bound to be a small table available this time of day. My journal called.

Settling into the familiar again, soaking up the atmosphere and the energy provided by the diverse clientele, I felt the comfort of home settle over me. *This is who I am. This is where I belong. I'm not a hockey fan. Heck, I'm not a sports fan. I'm not a party person. I'm not obsessed with my appearance and I'm not into fancy lingerie and exotically scented body lotion. I'm a literature-loving, coffee-shop-hanger-outer who happens to like Classic Vanilla lotion. I write. I think. I consider. I teach. I'm confidently single and, by golly, I keep a picture of a Greek beach under my blotter so I can plan my own vacations, thank you very much, which have everything to do with relaxing and nothing whatever to do with my job.*

Having run down the complete CV, I felt rejuvenated, re-established, reassured—momentarily. Then it occurred to me. Did Josh really ask me to be anyone other than who I am? Hadn't I done my very best to convince him I am not the very person I just claimed I like being? Am I so sure I like being her after all? Didn't I like how I felt in Lydia's little luxuries? And, didn't I like seeing Josh's face light up when he looked at me? Didn't I really enjoy those silly hockey games? I mean, no one was holding a gun to my head and forcing me to learn that the coach can pull the goalie to put an extra man on the ice or what the third-man-in rule was. No one had forced me to read *The Girl's Guide* and commit to memory the signals the officials use to call players on slashing, cross-checking, interference, and hooking, let alone what each of those little no-nos really looked like on the ice when a player executed one. Hadn't I felt alive in his presence, dining at fine restaurants? Even at that 50s-themed diner with the enormous yogurt parfait? Hadn't I enjoyed exploring the Patricia I hadn't known.

My coffee went cold. So did my blood. I had fallen in love. Not just with Josh Northshore, but with the Patricia Smythe I saw reflected in his eyes. I had tried on someone new and she was still me and I liked her.

I think, I'm going to miss being her.

"Hi." A too-perky voice brought me back to the present. "You haven't been in for a while." It was Zenobia. "Something's different."

"A new blend?" I asked, hoping for the best, but knowing this mystic young woman was reading my aura, or some other such nonsense, and was about to tell me something about myself I already knew I didn't want to hear.

"Your hair. You're wearing it down today instead of back."

"Yes," I said, and feeling laughter rising to my throat. I reached up and tucked a stray strand behind my ear. "Yes, I just thought, 'What the heck. Why not do something crazy today?'" Was I mocking her or me? It didn't matter. I had escaped with my aura intact.

"You're sad," she said, taking my hand and sitting down.

I shifted in my seat and looked around. The sight of two women holding hands was nothing that would cause eyebrows to raise around here, but I was uncomfortable nonetheless.

"What are you doing, Zenobia?" I asked, trying to pull back without making a scene.

"Your aura . . ."

Oh no.

"Your aura is depressed."

"It's a little humid today. My aura is always depressed when it's humid. Just like my hair." I forced a laugh.

She put her slender, pale hand across my eyes and mumbled something that sounded like Shakespeare in German. I gave in and sat still, waiting for lightning to strike.

"You're writing a wrong ending," she said, taking her hand away and looking me in the eye.

"What? This? Oh, this is a journal. It's not fiction."

"It's wrong."

"How can it be wrong? It's mine?"

"Nonetheless." Zenobia shrugged as if there was nothing further to discuss. She took my coffee cup and walked away humming a tune that sounded something like a lullabye.

I started to call to her attention that I wasn't yet fin-ished with my coffee and, by the way, had paid for the refillable cup. Instead, I looked at my laptop. The cursor blinked, waiting for some insightful phrase, some defining moment to be recorded. It could have blinked for eternity, but unless I got up and walked away, there would never be a chance to finish. It was too soon for conclusions.

I couldn't stop worrying about Abel. He had e-mailed me a very brief thank-you note after we returned. It read:

Miss Smythe,

Thank you for reading my essay and for everything you've done for me to help me get caught up. I know I didn't deserve it, so thank you. I hope that you at least had a good time on the trip. Sorry for all the trouble I caused. I'll see you next week (provided Josh lets me out of the house before my 21st birthday LOL).

Abel Northshore
PS: The Aerosmith concert was outstanding—thanks.

I responded:

Abel,

Thank you for being so serious about your studies and making it all worthwhile. I had a great time on the trip. I won't soon forget it. Thanks for all the hockey lessons! I hope things get back to normal for you at home. See you in the new semes-ter!

Miss Smythe

PS: Please tell your brother thank you and hello? PS: Please ask Josh to call me? PS: What am I going to do now?

Chapter Eleven

Looking around my living room, I was met with overwhelming evidence that I am afraid of failure, which explains my lack of self-confidence and avoidance of commitment.

One time, I had decided to paint my living room a very beautiful shade of brown. It was a soft, warm color, neutral enough to accommodate most furnishings but rich and deep. I painted one wall and became afraid that it would be too dark. So I quit. I rearranged the furniture so that the big, brown wall was mostly hidden by the entertainment center and a large plant. The rest of the room was eggshell, just as it had been when I moved in.

In the same room, on a high shelf, I have a very small collection of metal lunchboxes: "Charlie's Angels," "Sigmund and the Sea Monster," "H.R. Puff N Stuff," and

"The Muppet Show"—all programs I enjoyed as a kid. I liked them and they seemed an appropriate collection for a schoolteacher, but I was afraid they were too out of synch with the rest of my décor, so I stuck them up high and hadn't added to the collection for several years.

I decided to redecorate.

Impulsiveness is not a part of my bent, but I tore to the nearest home improvement store and pulled a dozen paint chips in various shades of greens and blues—reminiscent of the colors in the pictures of Greece I'd studied for so long. Next, I visited the discount store across the road and, chips in hand, pondered the endless selection of bedspreads and comforters. After settling on an off-white sateen comforter, I selected two beaded and tasseled little throw pillows. On my way back to the cash registers, I spotted a framed print called "Relax" of white Adirondack chairs facing the ocean from the porch of a weathered house.

With two cans of paint, a variety of brushes, paint stirrers, three large drop cloths, and a long-handled roller, I sucked in my breath and started.

It was Wednesday. By the time I returned to work, I would have the bedroom finished and maybe even the bathroom too.

Sometimes we get a picture of ourselves in our minds and we are so certain that this picture represents the truth of who we are that we give no credence to, allow no room for the possibility, that there are other possibilities for us, other selves to be explored. I happened to catch a glimpse of someone I liked in the eyes of someone else. I walked away and found myself, standing in the center of my dismantled and half-painted bedroom, afraid I couldn't go back.

I sat down in the middle of the nearest drop cloth and stared at the walls. When had I become so bland? Why had I ignored the prospect that my life didn't have to be what it had always been? When did I decide . . . wait. Did I decide? Or did I just fall in step like so many others who live, as Thoreau so poignantly put it, "lives of quiet desperation?" The paint on the walls was a decision. It was impetuous, but it was a decision. Going on that trip with Josh had been a decision too. Prior to that, though, when was the last real decision I'd made outside of what to have for supper or which television show to watch? I couldn't immediately recall; however, I think it probably was a few years ago when I decided to stay on as a teacher. I wasn't happy doing what I was doing. Contracts came out and I let mine set until the last minute—a thing I never do—before signing it and returning it. I remember the depression that seemed to settle over me then. I talked to myself a lot that summer. *Teaching is a worthwhile career.* And, it is. *This is what you trained to do. You're still paying student loans.* And, I am. *There are young people out there who can really benefit from having you in the classroom.* There are. But, the kicker question—the one without an answer—was what drove me to sign on the dotted line: *What else would I do?*

It wasn't for lack of imagination that I stayed. I have dreamed myself doing many other things in life. It was for lack of courage. My favorite pastime for about three years seemed to be updating my resume and perusing the classified ads. Not having a valid reason for leaving and not having a real offer to accept—those were my reasons for staying.

"I've become one of those people," I said aloud in the echoing room. "I'm one of those people who just fall into a life rather than making one."

I wandered into the living room and reached for the remote. The sportscasters' round and shining faces met me eye-to-eye as I stood there in the living room. There was some basketball game going on in the background. A ribbon under the screen advertised upcoming events to be broadcast. TONIGHT: ST. LOUIS SHOWBOATS AT CHICAGO BLACKHAWKS 7 P.M.

The doorbell rang. Nanna's shock registered immediately upon seeing me, paint roller in hand and smudges on my knuckles. I'm a messy painter.

"What in God's good name are you doing?" She set Bitsy down.

"Painting."

"Where?" She looked around the room.

"My bedroom."

"You're painting your bedroom? *This* color?" She touched a knuckle.

"Yes."

"You're painting your bedroom?" she asked again.

"No, actually, I'm not. I'm getting ready to take a little trip. How would you like to go to Chicago?" I smiled. I was giving into an impulse and, boy, did it feel good.

"I'd love to," Nanna said without hesitation.

There it was—decision. Nanna could do it. So could I.

"Okay. We leave in an hour. Get packed."

"How long will we be gone?"

"Just tonight."

"Right," Nanna said, clapping her hands together and regathering Bitsy.

"See you in an hour," I said, practically pushing her out the door.

"Oh, I forgot," she said, turning.

"What?"

"What should I bring?"

"Bring your gloves." I smiled and shut the door. There wasn't much time.

Driving with my grandmother has always been a trial. Initially, she's a chatterbox; ultimately, she's a sleeper. But she's a light sleeper. So, every truck that passes or any road noise will wake her with a start. Her arms flail about and she gasps like she can't breathe. If it doesn't drive you crazy, it can be rather funny. I've learned to anticipate this over the years and it doesn't bother me so much anymore. It does, however, bother Bitsy who takes a full mile's drive to calm down and go back to sleep.

"So," Nanna began innocently enough, "you've fallen in love."

It wasn't a question but a statement, which annoyed the daylights out of me.

"No, Nanna. I haven't fallen in love. I just thought that it would be nice to finish what I started."

"I thought you did that already," Nanna goaded. "You said Abel caught up on all his work and did great on his exam. Isn't that what you were doing?"

I glowered over the top of my sunglasses. "Feel free to doze off. I'm fine."

Nanna smiled smugly and turned toward the window. In the space of a few miles I could hear her breathing nice and evenly. A respite for the both of us. A few miles outside of Chicago, I phoned the hotel where I had originally been booked and discovered to my delight that the reservation had not been cancelled. I asked them to transfer the bill to my own credit card rather than that of Mr. Northshore and told them there would be an extra guest in the room. My grandmother has an unreasonable fear of hotels, no matter how nice they are.

"We're here," I said, shaking her gently.

"Already?" She yawned and stretched.

I popped the trunk open. "Why don't you take Bitsy over there and I'll get us checked in. We have time for a quick dinner before game time."

Fortunately, the team was already at the arena and there would be no chance of my running into Josh or any of the others. I called to Nanna, who had already taken up with another dog owner out by the flowerbeds.

"We're in four-twelve," I said.

"Be right up." She waved back. "This is Michelle. She's here on her honeymoon. And this is Calamity Jane." She indicated Michelle's schnauzer.

"CJ for short," Michelle called.

"Nice to meet you," I answered. "I'm going to grab a quick shower."

"I'll call room service," Nanna offered.

I left her and her new friends standing on the lawn. Digging through my hastily packed overnight bag, I cursed myself for leaving the Chai lotion in Seattle.

"Classic Vanilla will have to do," I said to myself, peering into the rapidly fogging mirror. "Good luck," I whispered.

The arena atmosphere was electric. The only color discernible in the whole place was red. Fans flocked in. There had been a copy of the *Tribune* in the room and I noticed a story which foretold a big win for the Blackhawks, who had beaten the Showboats the past six times they'd met on the ice. Ticket holders were all but guaranteed a victory for Chicago.

I traded my ticket on the ground level for two higher up. It wasn't so bad. The view of the ice was very different and as the game started, it looked less like scrambling and more like strategy than I had previously noticed.

"Pretty good vantage point," I remarked.

"I've never been to a hockey game before." Nanna sounded like a kid going to kindergarten.

"You'll like it," I said without taking my eyes from the ice. The teams had come out for their skate-around. "It's very physical." I elbowed her playfully.

With a full twenty minutes on the clock and the anthem already swallowed up in crowd noise, the starting lines took their places.

"Which one is he?" Nanna whispered.

"On the outside of the circle. About twelve-oh-five"— I pointed—"number twenty-two."

Chicago scored twice in the first ten minutes. The roar was deafening.

"They're not doing so great," Nanna whispered.

"They look a little sluggish. They've been on the road a while."

As the clock ran down to the end of the first period, a single player in blue skated out of the penalty box, and scored at the last second. We were losing, but not by much. There was hope.

"Goal for the Showboats by Lyle Sikes. Assist by Josh Northshore," the announcer stated matter-of-factly.

"Yes," I said under my breath.

The second period was intense. The shift changes were fast and furious; the penalties were few and far between. My heart was racing and my palms sweaty. I had become so involved in the game I had forgotten my real reason for driving all this way—what was to come after the game.

Coach pulled Samson when Chicago scored its third goal and Brickman took his place between the pipes.

"Seems a shame," Nanna said. "He's played the whole game and doesn't get to finish it."

"There's no room for error. He's probably tired. Look at the shots on goal." I pointed to the scoreboard.

"Is that what SOG is?" Nanna laughed. "I won't tell you what I thought that stood for."

Samson had already blocked five of six shots in a matter of minutes this period. Brickman looked fierce. He was bigger than Samson. I watched him crouch down, ready for business. The official's whistle blew and the face-off was at our goal end. Skywalker headed up the ice and passed the puck to Josh. I could see the team forming a narrow but long triangle near the goal. Each pass was excruciating. Finally we scored. I jumped to my feet before I knew what I was doing.

"Ah, sit down, lady," the man behind me said. "This is Chicago, okay. Windy City's gonna blow you away." He snorted and took a long draw on his draft.

"Score by Lyle Sikes with James Allen on the assist."

I sat down sheepishly and turned my attention back to the ice. The score was three-three with two minutes remaining in regulation. A mere two seconds after face-off and Skywalker was in the box for hooking. With Chicago on the power play, the whole crowd was on its feet. For nearly a full two minutes, the Showboats cleared their end of the ice, shooting the puck across the farthest blue line three times before I saw a beautiful sight. Brickman skated off and Josh came on as a sixth man. The breakaway took him straight to the crease for a winning goal.

I looked over my shoulder at the man with the beer and smiled sweetly. "Good game," I said.

"One outta seven, lady. One outta seven." He then drained his cup. "Wait 'til next time."

We hung back to let the crowd get ahead of us and drove slowly back to the hotel.

"What now?" Nanna asked.

"Now?"

"Yes. It's only ten."

"Ten o'clock in a strange city is like two o'clock at home."

"What's that supposed to mean?"

"It means you're going to the room and I'm going to take care of some business."

"Oh." I could see her knowing smile in the lights of oncoming traffic.

"Okay?"

"Okay."

I refreshed my makeup and rubbed a little more Classic Vanilla on my hands and neck for luck, bade Nanna good night, and went to the restaurant below. I hadn't been able to wring Josh's room number out of the desk clerk, so I thought my best chance at finding him was the restaurant. If he wasn't there, at least maybe one of the team would be and they could help me out.

As luck, or fate, or God, would have it, Lyle Sikes and James Allen entered the bar just ahead of me. I followed at a safe distance, scanning faces for familiarity. I couldn't see Josh anywhere. Skywalker and The Fist joined a few others at a table toward the back. I edged that way, waiting until the waitress had taken their drink orders before sliding up behind Lyle.

"Thought sure you'd have a hat trick tonight, Skywalker," I said.

"Teach!" Sikes shouted. "Good to see ya! Thought you'd gone back to school."

"Still have a few days left."

"Have a seat," someone else said and several men on the other side of the table started shifting to make room.

"Thanks. I was really looking for Josh. Is he coming down?"

"Don't know that he said," David Brickman considered.

"Think he'd talk to me?" I whispered the question by Brickman's ear as everyone else went about placing their orders.

"Room seven-twenty-eight," he said, winking at me and smiling warmly. I turned to go. "See you at the twins' party?"

"Hope so," I said and waved good-bye. "Good to see you all."

"See ya, Teach," Sikes called.

The elevator was empty. I pressed the button for the seventh floor with a cold, trembling finger. As the elevator started up, I had a sinking feeling. What if he wasn't happy to see me? What if I'd misread Brickman's response. Josh was a pretty private person. I doubt he's spoken to Brickman about me. I'm sure he was just being polite. Worse yet, what if he opened the door and there was someone else inside with him? Not Abel, but another woman? Not likely was it? I mean, I hadn't heard him mention anyone before. Besides, it hadn't been that long ago that he was dancing with me and kissing me good night. No, he wouldn't be with another woman. But, what if he wasn't there at all? Or, what if he was? What did I plan to say? Panic was setting in completely when the elevator arrived at the seventh floor. The doors opened. I stepped into the hallway and bumped into someone.

"Excuse me," I said, feeling more and more nauseated.

"Patricia?" Josh's voice registered a pleasing blend of confusion and delight. "What are you doing here?"

I looked up into his eyes. I had to find a place of stability before I fainted dead away.

"Looking for you," I said numbly.

"You found me." He reached out to take my arm. Did I look that unsteady?

"David told me your room number."

"I'm glad," he said, a slight smile bringing life and warmth to his face. "I'm very glad."

We walked the corridor without speaking. He opened the door to his room and I went in.

"Is Abel here?" I turned and asked suddenly.

"No. Why?"

"I don't know," I said, feeling very out of touch with reality.

"Are you okay?"

"I think so."

"Why don't you sit down?"

I sat on the sofa. He took the seat across from me and my heart sank. I looked at him there, sitting forward on the chair, leaning toward me, his hands turned upward in a kind of unasked question.

"Hi," I said.

"Hi."

"I wanted to talk to you," I began, shaking my head to try and clear some of the confusion that had settled in like a thick fog.

"I wanted to talk to you too."

"You did?"

"Yes. I've been missing you."

"You have?"

"Yes. In between dealing with things at home and trying to get my head back in the game for tonight. In those precious few quiet moments between . . . I have been missing you." His eyes searched mine. "I'm very sorry our trip ended the way it did."

"So, is Abel okay?"

Josh sat back in his chair. "I think so."

"I was just worried after all that happened. I wanted to make sure he was doing okay."

"And that's why you came to Chicago?"

"Well, that and I wanted to see you beat the Black-hawks."

"Which we did."

"Great game," I said, smiling.

"Yeah."

"So, Abel is okay, then?"

"Yeah, I'm sure he's fine. I mean, he's grounded for the rest of the school year, but other than that . . ."

"Good. I'm glad. I was worried."

"So you said." He smiled. "So, you got to see us win, you know that Abe's okay. What now?"

"Um, well, I guess I just wanted to say thank you."

"You're welcome. For what?"

"For the trip. The chance, really, to have a lot of fun over the break. Do some things I've never done before. See some places I might not have seen otherwise. Hear a carillon . . ." I felt myself warming on the inside.

"I'm glad you had fun."

"I did."

"I did too."

"Look, Josh, I know—" I didn't know. I didn't know anything. Right at this exact moment, I wasn't certain of anything at all, not even of my own name.

"Patricia?"

"Yes, Josh?"

He moved toward me. As he sat on the sofa next to me, my body leaned slightly toward his. He was close enough that I could feel his warmth, smell his scent, breathe his breath. I waited for his next words like I was waiting for my next heartbeat.

"Patricia." He moved closer.

His mouth, his perfect mouth, was next to my ear. I shivered. He wrapped his arms around me and held me tight. I felt a small, cold tear of relief trickle down my cheek when I knew he would kiss me. I watched as it fell onto the back of his hand. I raised my eyes to meet his. He lowered his mouth on mine and I fell off the face of the earth, floating away into the outer orbits of the universe, losing all sense of time and place, losing all sense of self. I raised my trembling hands to his face, desperate to anchor myself, to know that this was real. When our lips parted, I heard all that I thought I had known about life, about myself, go out of me in a tiny, nearly inaudible gasp. But Josh heard it. He heard it and answered it: "I'm so glad you came."

"I'm glad I came, too," I answered as unexpected and inexplicable laughter suddenly rose in my throat. I laughed until I cried. The tension of a lifetime of needing to know the answers to all the whys washed away in a cleansing wave of the ridiculous. What did it matter?

Josh laughed too. Though he was a man in the prime of his life, it was as if years melted from his face and we were lovers in the flush of youth. He wrapped his strong and protective arm around my shoulders and shut out the lights. We watched the stars shining down over the city, the moon pass through our small frame of reference, and the sun rise rosy red on a new day.

"I'm so happy," I whispered, breaking the silence of the contented hours spent in his embrace. "So happy."

He kissed me again and my life began.

A cheer went up when I entered the Fellowship Hall at LaFayette Community Church. This, I thought, must be how Josh feels when he skates out as part of the starting line.

"Pat in the Hat!" Jason called to me, smiling his broad, toothless smile and waving wildly. "How was Canada?"

"Great, Jason. Good to be back, though."

"Heard you joined the Brown Baggers the other day." Ruby, who always sounded accusatory no matter what she said, wagged a finger in my face.

"Don't worry, Ruby, no one could ever replace you in my heart." I squeezed her arm.

Coffee brimming in Styrofoam cups, the Crew, as they liked to be called, dragged folding chairs into a large circle at the center of the room and settled in. I began digging through my tote bag which bore the slogan, READY, SET, READ!, until I came up with a small gift bag.

"What'd you bring us?" Thomas, one of the Crew's younger members, asked, leaning forward and trying to peer down into the sack.

"Surprises."

"Wow!" Ruby exclaimed, clutching the red-beaded monogram bookmark to her chest. "It's beautiful! Thank you!"

I really felt like Santa now with my bag full of colorful, glittering goodies.

"For Thomas. For Sara. For Nora . . ." I finished my round and a hush fell over the group as they sat, admiring their gifts and looking to me as the clock struck seven. "Time to start," I announced, reaching back into my bag of tricks. "I thought we'd begin tonight with some informational brochures. I took one and passed the stack to Thomas who eagerly distributed them. "Read the brochure you receive. Remember to use visual clues to help with meaning: Charts, maps, photos. Also, we talked about text supports: Headings, subheadings, insets. Be prepared to summarize the content and share a section with the group."

I excused myself to get some coffee as my eager readers attacked their projects.

"Great idea," Hillary whispered.

"When did you come in?" I asked, surprised to see her.

"I was just passing by and I saw a young man standing out front looking like he couldn't decide whether or not to come in." She stepped aside and I saw Abel in the foyer, head down and shuffling his feet.

"Abel?" I asked, stepping into the lobby.

"I'll fill in," Hillary offered.

"Thanks."

"Sorry to bother you, Miss Smythe," he began. "I shouldn't have come."

"No, Abel, don't be silly. Is everything okay? Are you okay?"

He looked ill. "I'm okay."

"Is it Josh? Is he okay?"

Abel looked me in the eye then, confusion quickly turning to amusement. "Josh is fine. Why?" His teasing tone took me by surprise and my defenses went up immediately.

"No reason." I shrugged but he was still smiling broadly. "What is it, then?" I was losing my patience.

"I just wanted to apologize." His smile was completely gone now.

"I got your e-mail, Abel. All's forgiven. If there even was anything to forgive in the first place. I guess your brother let you out before your twenty-first birthday after all, huh? He does know you're here?" I felt a sudden sense of alarm.

"Yeah. Well, he doesn't know I'm *here* here, but he knows I'm out."

"Good. Well, anyway, if that's all you wanted, to apologize, it's all fine. Okay?" I extended my hand toward him, but he was looking down again.

"It's not *all* I wanted," he mumbled.

"Oh?"

"I don't want to bother you, though. You're busy and I really should be going. So, just forget it." He turned to leave.

"Whoa," I said, grabbing hold of his elbow. "Hold it. You don't get off that easy. What's up?"

"I really didn't mean to bother you." He was embarrassed. "What's that group anyway? Are you in AA?"

His face seemed to brighten as he exercised his good-natured teenage derision.

"This is a literacy group."

"Oh." He didn't know what to make of that. Peeking over my shoulder, he could see the Crew in its huddle.

"Not what you'd expect is it?"

"No. Not really." He looked more closely.

I turned to try seeing them through his eyes: A dozen or so people my age, his brother's age, and older, seated in metal chairs, nursing coffee and discussing the Space Needle, Pike's Market, and gourmet coffees, not from firsthand experience, but as experienced through the written word. Abel stepped past me to the door and leaned in. I followed.

"Which text supports helped you the most, Ruby?" Hillary asked.

"This list. Here." Ruby held up her brochure to show the group.

"And what was it about the list that was so helpful?" Hillary probed.

Ruby turned the brochure back to herself to consider the question. Before she answered, Abel turned back to me. His face registered disbelief as another bright thread in the tapestry of innocence broke.

"They're old," he said.

I laughed. "Older, yes," I corrected. "Some my age. Some older. One"—I leaned in and pointed to Thomas—"not many years older than you. There."

He shook his head, amazed. "Cool."

"Yeah, it's cool. But, back to you, Abel. What did you want? Besides to apologize?"

We stood facing each other, straining to see eye to eye across a thick and sturdy wall of years and fears.

"Josh told me you came to see him in Chicago."

"Yes?"

"Well, I just wanted to tell you that it's okay."

"What's okay?"

"It's okay with me that you're . . ."

Light was dawning. He was embarrassed.

"That I'm what?"

"It's okay with me that you're with my brother," he rushed through the sentence to its end. I could see the release register on his face. "Except—" Turning his eyes back to mine, I could see the earnest apprehension lurking behind the blue pools.

"Except . . ." I prodded. He remained silent. "It's okay, Abel. You can tell me. You're allowed to say whatever it is you're thinking. It won't hurt my feelings." I heard the words coming out of my mouth, but in my heart I was feeling very afraid.

Josh and I had agreed to pursue our relationship despite the obvious drawbacks of Abel still being my student and the hockey season still several weeks from its end. Before leaving Chicago, we had determined that, with school resuming the next week, we would see each other whenever the Showboats were scheduled for a home stand, and there were several remaining. We all would go about our daily business of school and study and practice and cooking and cleaning and literacy groups and whatever else each one of us did. Josh would tell Abel that he was seeing me *casually*—a word we agreed would be both an appropriate and palatable descriptor—and when May rolled around we would see if we—Josh and I—were ready to pursue things a little further. In the meantime, I was reading a new Grisham novel, painting my kitchen cupboards a lovely shade of green, and focusing on poetry instead of my journal.

"Except, Josh is really . . ." He hesitated again, his apprehension seeming to turn to outright fear.

"Josh is really what?" Now I was feeling uneasy. My brain began supplying an abundance of negative adjectives: *Mean, demanding, manipulative, violent, hardheaded . . . oh, what's that other word?*

"Really old." Having spoken his peace, Abel's face relaxed and his breathing returned to normal.

"Old?" I laughed.

"Yeah. He's, like, way older than you."

"Well, thank you, Abel, for your concern, but I don't think your brother is really that old. I am over thirty, you know." I laughed again.

"Oh, I know that," he said sincerely.

Taken down a notch, I forced a smile.

"It's not that he's that much older in years than you. It's just that you're kind of, well . . . you're younger in a kind of spiritual way."

"What's that mean?" I hoped that what sounded like a compliment would not turn out to be another back-door insult.

"Just that you are really, like, excited about things. You talk about how stuff relates to today, not just yesterday and you're all about the future. I don't know. I just think that Josh is kind of old that way. It's like he is very narrow. He sees things his way and that's it."

"I think I understand. Well, maybe between the two of us, we can open his mind a little bit. Do you think?"

"I don't know. He's pretty stubborn."

Stubborn! That's it! Stubborn! "Well, he kind of has to be. It's his business, isn't it?"

"I guess."

"Anyway, don't worry about it. We're just seeing each other *casually,* and I promise I won't let on at school so no one has to know but you and me. Okay?"

"Sure," he said, his eyes drifting back to the crew. They had taken a break from brochures and were hitting the cookies.

"Would you like to come in? See what it's all about?"

"Nah." But he didn't move away from the door.

"Come on. No one will mind. You could read aloud to them for me."

His interest was piqued. "Really?"

"My throat's been a little scratchy tonight," I fibbed. "It would be a help to me if you would."

"Okay."

We went inside and Abel helped himself to a cookie.

"By the way, Abel," I whispered. "Thanks."

"You're welcome," he said, grinning proudly.

"Everyone," I announced, "I'd like you to meet Abel Northshore."

Abel offered a small, inconspicuous wave.

"Northshore like the Showboats player Northshore?"

"My brother," Abel said, suppressing his pride.

"Awesome," Thomas said, shaking his hand. "I'm Thomas."

"Hi."

"I'm having a little trouble with a sore throat tonight, so Abel has agreed to read for me."

"What's the story tonight?" Ruby asked.

"Well, we have a choice." I reached into the bag. "We can do a short story, or we can start a chapter book. I have Mark Twain's *The Notorious Jumping Frog of Calavaras County* or *A Separate Peace* by John Knowles."

"Oh, I loved that book," Abel said.

"Any objections?" I asked the Crew, handing the book to Abel.

"Go for it." Jason cast his vote and the rest of the Crew settled in to listen.

"Go ahead." I nodded to Abel who opened the book.

"Chapter One . . ." he began as I reached over and lovingly placed the comical red-and-white-striped hat like a crown atop his head.

Chapter Twelve

March came in like a lamb, but my impatience with the hockey season was like a lion. When Josh returned to St. Louis for the last home stand of the season, he called on me. That's what my grandmother calls it. He picked me up in his powder-blue Mustang, catching me off-guard on a Thursday evening, finding me covered in paint flecks and clad in ripped jeans and a flannel shirt. After a once-over with turpentine and a quick shower, I was ready. He drove me to the Loop.

"Did you remember your gloves?" he asked me, feeding the meter.

"Sure did." I pulled on the red-and-white-striped mittens and waved my hands in the air.

"Have I ever told you how sexy you look in those?" he whispered in my ear.

"No," I said, batting my eyes. "Do I?"

"Oh, baby, there's nothing as exciting as a woman in mittens."

I laughed and socked him in the arm. "Where are we going?"

"Well, I thought you might like a little fondue." He smirked.

"I haven't had any fondue for a while."

"Let's go, then."

We walked slowly. Evening had fallen and the lights of University City gleamed ahead of us. The dome of the synagogue and the columns at the entry made for a striking scene. The smell of incense was heavy in the air as we passed the record shop and a live band was playing at Blueberry Hill, their retro riffs electrifying the air. Through the windows we could see an attentive and appreciative audience swilling sodas and tapping their feet. People wrapped up against the cold bustled in and out of shops and restaurants. Though I'd seen them a million times before, I took note of the stars laid in the sidewalk, reading their names aloud as we went: Kate Chopin, Miles Davis, Agnes Moorehead.

"Where's yours?" I nudged Josh.

"Right there." He paused and pointed to a bright star above the steeple of a nearby church. "That one's mine. Make a wish."

I closed my eyes and offered more of a prayer than a wish.

"What did you ask for?" he whispered hopefully.

"I'll tell you when it comes true." I laughed.

"I hope that's soon." He offered his arm.

"So do I," I answered, snuggling in close.

We walked the rest of the way in comfortable silence. When we arrived at the restaurant, I noticed there were no other customers inside.

"Are they open?" I asked Josh who was taking my coat.

His answer was nothing more than a wink and a smile.

"Mr. Northshore," the host greeted him warmly. "We have your table ready." He gestured to the same table Josh and I had the first time we were out together.

"Thank you," Josh said and pressed his hand into the small of my back, steering me to the intimate table by the window we had shared the last time we had come to the Loop, when everything had been decorated for Christmas. It seemed so long ago and yet, it seemed like only yesterday.

I slid into my seat and saw that there was a scroll tied with a red-and-white-striped ribbon set at my place. Josh seated himself and smiled at me across the candlelit table.

"What's this?" I asked, picking it up. "New menu?"

"Open it."

I slid the ribbon off the rolled-up parchment and laid it aside. My hands were suddenly trembling. Something about the whole scene was uncertain, yet wonderfully so. Josh's eyes were glued on my face. I could feel his excitement; it was as palpable as the scent of sweet and savory spices mingling in the air. I unrolled the scroll and read:

My Darling, Patricia, with your cold little hands, You warm my heart with your smile. I love you. I've not been the same since the day we met. I've been better.

Thank you.

My eyes teared up so I couldn't see. I felt Josh's hand cover mine.

"Will you celebrate with me?" he whispered.

"Celebrate?"

"Celebrate us?"

"Of course, I will," I said, reaching across the table.

"It's been three months since we met," he said.

"Three months? Is that all?"

He kissed my hand.

"This is what I wished," I whispered in his ear. "That's some quick wishing star you've got."

"This is only the beginning."

When the waitress served us the last steaming pot of chocolate, we lingered over cubes of angel cake and strawberries until the kitchen staff began cleaning up. Reluctant to let it end, we headed a little farther up the street, stopping in front of City Hall. We sat on the cold stone steps and looked at the sky.

"Patricia," he said softly.

"Yes," I said, snuggling in.

"It's a beautiful name." He kissed my hair.

I laughed. "Josh, this is more happiness than I ever dreamed possible for me."

He chuckled, embarrassed.

"No, really." I gushed, "You are the prince of the fairy tales, the hero of some ancient fable . . ."

"You're talking like a teacher." He lightly pressed the tip of my nose with his fingertip.

"I just can't get over it," I said shaking my head. "Of all the scenarios I imagined for my life, all the multiple choice tests I've arranged to help me make decisions, to determine my future, I never conceived of you."

"Thank goodness senior English is a graduation requirement," he said solemnly.

"Thank goodness."

The end of school is such a busy time, but besides the usual stacks of papers to grade and a new romance to tend to, there were celebrations as well. The Brickman girls turned eight with as much fanfare as the concurrent Stanley Cup celebration.

David and Sarah Brickman had a beautiful home. Sarah, a warm and wonderful person and a very attentive hostess, had outdone herself. I took over serving up the cake and ice cream so she could snap a few pictures and get everyone settled in for karaoke.

"Will you be singing?" Brickman asked, snagging a cup of punch.

"Not me." I shook my head vigorously. "You?"

"Not so much." He laughed. "Are you ready for summer?"

"Yes. If I can get through final exams then everything will be fine."

"You'll do it. You're a multitasker from way back." He grinned.

"How do you know?"

"Call it intuition?"

"Oh, sorry, I only accept intuitive recommendations from the girl at the coffee shop."

"Zenobia?"

"That's her!" I laughed. "You too?"

"Yeah, last time I talked to her, she told me not to let splashes ruin the day." He shrugged. "Got any clues on that one?"

"Not a clue."

Suddenly there was a wailing from the picnic table. One of the twins stood in her pale yellow eyelet-lace dress with a giant purple splotch on the front. Sarah was busily dabbing up the spill and Brickman encircled his daughter with his arms, drying tears and stroking her hair.

"No, that couldn't be it," I said out loud.

"What?" Josh appeared beside me. "Couldn't be what?"

"Oh, something Brickman said." I disregarded it, but remembered what Zenobia had last said to me about my ending not being finished. "Nothing," I repeated with assurance. "Did you get some cake?" I offered him a corner piece.

"You're beautiful," he said, setting the cake aside and wrapping his arms around me. "Absolutely beautiful."

"What do you think of the house?" Josh asked.

"It's beautiful."

"Have you ever been to Springfield?"

"Illinois?"

"No, Missouri," he said, taking up his cake again.

"No, why?"

"They've built a new ice rink there. Bringing in a minor league team."

"Really? That's interesting." I wasn't sure of the relevance of the conversation.

"They have some really beautiful homes there. Old homes with all the nooks and crannies and character."

"Cracking walls, you mean?"

"Tall trees, flowering shrubs. Revitalized downtown."

"Are you writing a brochure for their chamber of commerce?" I asked.

"Would you like to go sometime? They have a carillon there."

"Sure. I like the carillon."

"Might make an appointment with a real estate agent."

"Why would you do that?"

"You know I'm old, right?"

"Older. By comparison and only by industry standards."

"Yes, well, nonetheless."

"What are you driving at, Mr. Northshore?" I was feeling a black suspicion growing in me. "Exactly?"

"Retiring," he said quickly.

"Retiring?"

"Moving to Springfield. Coaching the new team."

"Retiring from playing?" I was incredulous. I knew it would come one day but not so soon.

"Yes." He leaned toward me to privatize the conversation. "What do you think?"

"I don't know. Retiring?"

"Retiring. What if I asked you to come along?" He reached down and took my left hand in his.

"That might be a bit presumptuous," I said, smiling at his purposefully obvious hint.

"Yes."

"I'd have to find a new job. Get tenured all over again."

"Or try something new? Write? I'm sure they need literacy instructors in Springfield. Be brave for me?" he asked, an achingly soft pleading in his eyes. "I really want this."

"You do?" I wasn't so sure. "You really want this?"

"I do."

"I do too." Courageous moves were not my modus operandi, but how could I say no to the man I cared for so much? How could I deny him pursuit of something new? And myself for that matter?

A world of new opportunities had started to open up before me as Sarah and her daughters sang "Somewhere

Over the Rainbow" at the karaoke machine. At least I wouldn't be alone.

The familiar strains of "Pomp and Circumstance" always bring a lump to my throat. I don't know why, really. Usually, I am working graduation. My favorite job is helping the grads line up in the back room before they march out. There's a palpable excitement in that room. It's bittersweet. They have come so far to arrive at this moment. They have so far to go to the next moment, yet they are blissfully unaware that they are crossing out of a space to which access will close forever once they walk out that door. They cross the threshold two by two. I watch them go and I feel proud of them, of myself, of the whole system of education; I feel sick-sad at the permanency of the closing doors.

Having given my resignation, I had been granted leave of my duties. I declined the offer. Of all the years I'd done this, of all the graduates I'd seen pass before me in this room, somehow it wouldn't be complete were I not there when Abel passed by. I would get to see him from a different vantage point than Josh. He should envy me that. I would join him in the auditorium afterward for the rest of the ceremony. This, though, was a most precious moment for teachers and students.

"Miss Smythe." Abel's teasing voice fell on my ear. He tapped my shoulder lightly.

"Abel, you look wonderful," I gushed and restrained myself from hugging him.

He looked taller in his cap and gown. A man.

"Thanks," he spoke softly.

"Congratulations," I said, regaining control of my emotions. "You worked hard."

"Not as hard as I should have"—he grinned—"but I had a lot of help."

"You'd better find your row." I nudged him in the direction of the noisy gym.

"You're coming to dinner after, right?"

"Of course." I beamed. "I wouldn't miss it."

"Great." He turned to go.

"Abel."

"Yeah?"

"Happy graduation."

"Thanks."

He was off to join the throng of jostling, posturing, giggling graduates all teetering between childhood and something beyond it which they didn't yet understand and couldn't quite get a handle on. I felt tears in my eyes just as the first strains of "Pomp and Circumstance" floated in over the commotion.

"Here we go," shouted someone at the front. "Class of 2009!"

A mighty cheer went up and just as quickly vanished in a sudden solemnity as the doors were opened and the first pair of graduates stepped through. They disappeared from sight slowly, steadily, until at last they were gone and the solid doors closed behind them, sealing them out of the past and into the future.

Rounding the corner, I scanned Section G, looking for Josh. I saw him straining to identify Abel, camera poised. Pride radiated from him.

"Have you spotted him?" I asked.

"Not yet." He didn't remove his eyes from the entry-way.

"He should be on this side. Maybe ten or twelve rows back. There"—I pointed—"see him? He's just walking in."

"Yes." Josh smiled broadly and aimed the camera quickly.

"Does he know where you're sitting?" I whispered.

Josh didn't have to answer. Just at that moment, Abel looked up and flashed a picture-perfect smile our way. The wait was interminable, but at last we heard his name echoing out over the crowd: "Abel Joseph Northshore." At that, I saw what must have felt like a lifetime of tension vanish from Josh's face. His easy smile and carefree laugh were winsome, but I hadn't realized before just how much anguish they covered. Abel was eighteen now, a high school graduate, and though he was many years away from being fully grown up and self-reliant, Josh—his brother, his guardian—must have believed that he was in many ways himself graduating. Given sole responsibility for the care and nurture of his little brother, he had seen him, pushed him, pulled him to this first of many milestones. They were closer now to being equals than they had ever been in their lives. He had reason to be proud.

Later, at the restaurant, with a few friends gathered to celebrate him, Abel was bombarded with the typical questions every person must suffer and ultimately answer. As the first barrage hit, I saw Abel's face light up and he stood.

"Hi, Hillary," he said.

"Hillary?" I asked, turning in my seat.

"Congratulations, Abel," she said, giving him a warm, motherly hug. "You looked so handsome in your cap and gown."

"Thanks," Abel said as he slid across the seat to make room.

"Hi, Patricia," Hillary said. "Is this your brother?" she asked Abel.

"Hillary Rispoliti, this is my brother, Josh Northshore."

"Nice to meet you." Josh half-stood and took Hillary's hand.

"Hillary's a literacy coach," I offered.

"Abel's training to take over a class on his own." She smiled and patted him on the back.

"Really?" I was stunned.

"Yes, really. You should be very proud of this young man." She looked Josh squarely in the face. "He's got a real gift and passion for helping our clients."

"I am proud," Josh answered. "Is this where you've been going on Tuesday nights?"

"Yeah, and Fridays."

"Fridays too?"

"Where did you think I was going?"

"Dates?" Josh said hopefully.

"Dates?" Abel laughed. "With the goofy girls from my school? No thanks."

"Not to worry," I interjected. "You'll meet plenty of girls who share your interests at the university."

Josh nodded and resumed his dinner.

"Yeah," Abel stammered and Hillary nodded at him and smiled. "Well, that will have to wait for a while."

"Wait?" Josh nearly choked. "Wait for what?"

"Wait for me. I'm going to work for the literacy council full-time for a while."

"Those are volunteer jobs, Abel," I reasoned while Josh took a long drink of water.

"Mostly, yes," Hillary concurred. "However, when a bright, young volunteer comes in and makes such a difference in the program *and* writes *and* wins a grant for ten thousand dollars for said program . . . well, need I say more?"

"Grant?" Josh stared, puzzled.

"A grant for ten thousand dollars for the literacy program?" I was astonished.

"We're going to use it to start an outreach to high school dropouts and graduates who somehow managed to slip through unnoticed"—he beamed—"like Thomas."

"Like Thomas." Hillary nodded in my direction. "It's a very worthwhile cause, Mr. Northshore, I hope you understand. There is no way I can even begin to convey to you the time and energy Abel has devoted to this program since, well, since February when he first wandered in to talk to you, Patricia."

Josh looked at me wide-eyed, then back to Abel. "No college?"

"Not right now. But don't worry. I'm all set up for an apartment just a few blocks from the church. It's all good."

"It's all good," Josh repeated suspiciously.

"I'm very pleased to know you're working there, Abel," I said. "That group has been a source of pure joy for me. I'm glad they'll have you around when I'm gone."

"I'm proud of you, Abe," Josh said.

"For graduating." Abel finished what he thought were Josh's thoughts.

"Yes, but more for finding something worthy of your energy, your enthusiasm. You'll do great. I know you will."

"Thanks, Josh"—Abel beamed—"thanks a lot."

On June 27, when the Stanley Cup excitement and hockey had been put safely behind us for a few months, Josh and I became officially engaged. Summer had arrived as suddenly as a breakaway goal—(*Oh, yes, I am beginning to use hockey similes quite frequently now*)— and so had true love. Orange day lilies and big, fluffy hydrangea blooms came back to life; I, too, was re-emerging, tender and new, after a long winter.

Life, as Nanna says, is all about trying. It's true, I guess, though I never knew it before. For me, life had always been about succeeding, about knowing things for certain. The only thing I knew undoubtedly that bright, beautiful morning of our engagement party was that I was in love with a wonderful man and that he loved me too. Nothing else mattered—nothing save that.

Standing before the mirror, smoothing on a hint of tinted lip gloss and applying a refreshing spritz of Chai body spray, I took a good long look at myself. Something was different. It wasn't just the dress—I had chosen a tea-length robin's egg-blue with a Nehru collar and a single pearl button in which to greet my guests. I leaned in to consider. Emily Dickinson said hope was a feathered thing alighting on a person's soul, ceaselessly singing a song without words. I think that hope is what I saw reflected there again: Lasting hope, hope enough to see me through the rest of my life, hope to begin afresh in a new city, hope enough to build a marriage on.

Josh wanted to worry about leaving Abel behind, but Nanna had found her soul mate in my former student. She and Mr. O'Malley parted ways for good—he must have changed his mind about dancing—and she'd taken a shine to Abel. She says he reminds her of her kid brother, my Great-uncle Dale whose legendary exploits have, I suspect, as much truth in them as any good tall tale. Abel doesn't mind Nanna's attention, though. She made him promise to come to dinner once a week. I hope he's got a strong stomach.

Springfield seems a lovely place. Josh and I fell in love with a charming home near the campus of Missouri

State. Lots of old trees in the yard, a park nearby, and plenty of the promised nooks and crannies to fill with hockey memorabilia and metal lunchboxes. The walls are all eggshell but paint isn't too expensive.

In every woman's life there comes a time when she must determine that true love is either worth waiting for or it isn't. If it is, she must bravely approach each day with the bright optimism of her youth, certain that this is the day she will be given that great gift she has been waiting for; if it isn't, she must choose to arrange a life for herself, one which she deems valuable enough to sustain her in her solitude. I arranged that life a million years ago, and I happily abandoned it the day I agreed to become Mrs. Josh Northshore.